CLUB SHADOWLANDS

MASTERS OF THE SHADOWLANDS
BOOK 1

CHERISE SINCLAIR

VanScoy Publishing Group

Club Shadowlands
Copyright © 2013 by Cherise Sinclair
ISBN : 978-1-947219-45-8
Published by VanScoy Publishing Group
Cover Artist: Christine M. Griffin & April Martinez

TO MY READERS

The books I write are fiction, not reality, and as in most romantic fiction, the romance is compressed into a very, very short time period.

You, my darlings, live in the real world, and I want you to take a little more time in your relationships. Good Doms don't grow on trees, and there are some strange people out there. So while you're looking for that special Dom, please, be careful.

When you find him, realize he can't read your mind. Yes, frightening as it might be, you're going to have to open up and talk to him. And you listen to him, in return. Share your hopes and fears, what you want from him, what scares you spitless. Okay, he may try to push your boundaries a little—he's a Dom, after all—but you will have your safe word. You will have a safe word, am I clear? Use protection. Have a back-up person. Communicate.

Remember: safe, sane, and consensual.

Know that I'm hoping you find that special, loving person who will understand your needs and hold you close.

And while you're looking or even if you have already found

your dearheart, come and hang out with the Masters of the Shadowlands.

Love,

Cherise

CHAPTER ONE

Jessica Randall scrambled out of the water-filled ditch, her heart hammering. Frigid rain slashed through the dark night, drenching her face and clothing. Gasping for breath, she knelt in the mud, surprised to have made it to the bank in one piece. She glanced over her shoulder and shuddered. Alligators loved to hang out in Florida ditches. A few moments more and she could have been... She stifled the thought with a shudder.

Hands shaking, she scrubbed the water off her face and pushed to her feet.

As her fear diminished, she peered through the darkness and could barely see her car. Poor little Taurus, nose down with water roiling around the hood.

"I'll be back for you. Don't worry," she promised, feeling as if she were abandoning her baby.

Once on the narrow country road, she pushed her tangled hair out of her face and looked each way. Darkness and darkness. Dammit, why couldn't she have an accident right in someone's front yard? But no, the nearest house was probably the one she'd passed about a mile back. She headed that way, stopping to glare at the pool of water where her car had aquaplaned right off the

1

road. The armadillo, of course, was long gone. At least she hadn't hit it.

Head lowered, she trudged down the blacktop toward the house, getting wetter and wetter. Hopefully she wouldn't trip on something in the darkness. Breaking her leg would be the final straw in a day that had been a disaster from start to finish.

Number one mistake: meeting at a halfway point for their first date when the man lived miles and miles outside of Tampa.

He sure hadn't been worth the trip. She'd have found more excitement auditing business accounts. Then again, he hadn't appeared all that impressed with her either. She grimaced. She'd recognized the look in his eyes, the one that said he really wanted tall and slim, an Angelina Jolie type woman, no matter that her posted picture portrayed her quite accurately: a pint-size Marilyn Monroe.

So far, she'd have to say finding a guy through the Internet rated right up there with back-country shortcuts, her second mistake of the day.

Aunt Eunice always swore things happened in threes. So would braking for an armadillo be considered her third mistake, or was there another disaster lurking in her near future?

She shivered as the wind howled through the palmettos and plastered her drenched clothing against her chilled body. Couldn't stop now. Doggedly, she set one foot in front of the other, her waterlogged shoes squishing with every step.

An eternity later, she spotted a glimmer of light. Relief rushed through her when she reached a driveway studded with hanging lights. Surely whoever lived here would let her wait out the storm. She walked through the ornate iron gates, up the palm-lined drive past landscaped lawns, until finally she reached a three-story stone mansion. Black wrought iron lanterns illuminated the entry.

"Nice place," she muttered. And a little intimidating. She glanced down at herself to check the damage. Mud and rain streaked her tailored slacks and white button-down shirt, hardly a suitable image for a conservative accountant. She looked more like something even a cat would refuse to drag in.

Shivering hard, she brushed at the dirt and grimaced as it only streaked worse. She stared up at the huge oak doors guarding the entrance. A small doorbell in the shape of a dragon glowed on the side panel, and she pushed it.

Seconds later, the doors opened. A man, oversized and ugly as a battle-scarred Rottweiler, looked down at her. "I'm sorry, miss, you're too late. The doors are locked."

What the heck did that mean?

"P-please," she said, stuttering with the cold. "My car's in a ditch, and I'm soaked, and I need a place to dry out and call for help." But did she really want to go inside with this scary-looking guy? Then she shivered so hard her teeth clattered together, and her mind was made up. "Can I come in? Please?"

He scowled at her, his big-boned face brutish in the yellow entry light. "I'll have to ask Master Z. Wait here." And the bastard shut the door, leaving her in the cold and dark.

Jessica wrapped her arms around herself, standing miserably, and finally the door opened again. Again the brute. "Okay, come on in."

Relief brought tears to her eyes. "Thank you, oh, thank you." Stepping around him before he could change his mind, she barreled into a small entry room and slammed into a solid body. "Oomph," she huffed.

Firm hands gripped her shoulders. She shook her wet hair out of her eyes and looked up. And up. The guy was big, a good six feet, his shoulders wide enough to block the room beyond.

He chuckled, his hands gentling their grasp on her arms. "She's freezing, Ben. Molly left some clothing in the blue room; send one of the subs."

"Okay, boss." The brute—Ben—disappeared.

"What is your name?" Her new host's voice was deep, dark as the night outside.

3

"Jessica." She stepped back from his grip to get a better look at her savior. Smooth black hair, silvering at the temples, just touching his collar. Dark gray eyes with laugh lines at the corners. A lean, hard face with the shadow of a beard adding a hint of roughness. He wore tailored black slacks and a black silk shirt that outlined hard muscles underneath. If Ben was a Rottweiler, this guy was a jaguar, sleek and deadly.

"I'm sorry to have bothered—" she started.

Ben reappeared with a handful of golden clothing that he thrust at her. "Here you go."

She took the garments, holding them out to keep from getting the fabric wet. "Thank you."

A faint smile creased the manager's cheek. "Your gratitude is premature, I fear. This is a private club."

"Oh. I'm sorry." Now what was she going to do?

"You have two choices. You may sit out here in the entryway with Ben until the storm passes. The forecast stated the winds and rain would die down around six or so in the morning, and you won't get a tow truck out on these country roads until then. Or you may sign papers and join the party for the night."

She looked around. The entry was a tiny room with a desk and one chair. Not heated. Ben gave her a dour look.

Sign something? She frowned. Then again, in this lawsuit-happy world, every place made a person sign releases, even to visit a fitness center. So she could sit here all night. Or...be with happy people and be warm. *No-brainer.* "I'd love to join the party."

"So impetuous," the manager murmured. "Ben, give her the paperwork. Once she signs—or not—she may use the dressing room to dry off and change."

"Yes, sir." Ben rummaged in a file box on the desk, pulled out some papers.

The manager tilted his head at Jessica. "I will see you later then."

Ben shoved three pages of papers at her and a pen. "Read the

4

rules. Sign at the bottom." He scowled at her. "I'll get you a towel and clothes."

She started reading. *Rules of the Shadowlands.*

"Shadowlands. That's an unusual na—" she said, looking up. Both men had disappeared. Huh. She returned to reading, trying to focus her eyes. Such tiny print. Still, she never signed anything without reading it.

Doors will open at...

Water pooled around her feet, and her teeth chattered so hard she had to clench her jaw. There was a dress code. Something about cleaning the equipment after use. Halfway down the second page, her eyes blurred. Her brain felt like icy slush. *Too cold—I can't do this.* This was just a club, after all; it wasn't like she was signing mortgage papers.

Turning to the last page, she scrawled her name and wrapped her arms around herself. *Can't get warm.*

Ben returned with some clothing and towels, then showed her into an opulent restroom off the entry. Glass-doored stalls along one side faced a mirrored wall with sinks and counters.

After dropping the borrowed clothing on the marble counter, she kicked her shoes off and tried to unbutton her shirt. Something moved on the wall. Startled, Jessica looked up and saw a short, pudgy woman with straggly blonde hair and a pale complexion blue with cold. After a second, she recognized herself. *Ew.* Surprising they'd even let her in the door.

In a horrible contrast with Jessica's appearance, a tall, slender, absolutely gorgeous woman walked into the restroom and gave her a scowl. "I'm supposed to help you with a shower."

Get naked in front of Miss Perfection? Not going to happen. "Thanks, b-b-b-but I'm all right." She forced the words past her chattering teeth. "I don't need help."

"Well!" With an annoyed huff, the woman left.

I was rude. Shouldn't have been rude. If only her brain would kick back into gear, she'd do better. She'd have to apologize. Later. If she ever got dried off and warm. She needed dry clothes. But, her hands were numb, shaking uncontrollably, and time after time, the buttons slipped from her stiff fingers. She couldn't even get her slacks off, and she was shuddering so hard her bones hurt.

"Dammit," she muttered and tried again.

The door opened. "Jessica, are you all right? Vanessa said—" The manager. "No, you are obviously not all right." He stepped inside, a dark figure wavering in her blurry vision.

"Go away."

"And find you dead on the floor in an hour? I think not." Without waiting for her answer, he stripped her out of her clothes as one would a two-year-old, even peeling off her sodden bra and panties. His hands were hot, almost burning, against her chilled skin.

She was naked. As the thought percolated through her numb brain, she jerked away and grabbed at the dry clothing. His hand intercepted hers.

"No, pet." He plucked something from her hair, opening his hand to show muddy leaves. "You need to warm up and clean up. Shower."

He wrapped a hard arm around her waist and moved her into one of the glass-fronted stalls behind where she'd been standing. With his free hand, he turned on the water, and heavenly warm steam billowed up. He adjusted the temperature.

"In you go," he ordered. A hand on her bottom, he nudged her into the shower.

The water felt scalding hot against her frigid skin, and she gasped, then shivered, over and over, until her bones hurt. Finally, the heat began to penetrate, and the relief was so intense, she almost cried.

Some time after the last shuddering spasm, she realized the door of the stall was open. Arms crossed, the man leaned against the door frame, watching her with a slight smile on his lean face.

"I'm fine," she muttered, turning so her back was to him. "I can manage by myself."

"No, you obviously cannot," he said evenly. "Wash the mud out of your hair. The left dispenser has shampoo."

Mud in her hair. She'd totally forgotten; maybe she *did* need a keeper. After using the vanilla-scented shampoo, she let the water sluice through her hair. Brown water and twigs swirled down the drain. The water finally ran clear.

"Very good." The water shut off. Blocking the door, he rolled up his sleeves, displaying corded, muscular arms. She had the unhappy feeling he was going to keep helping her, and any protest would be ignored. He'd taken charge as easily as if she'd been one of the puppies at the shelter where she volunteered.

"Out with you now." When her legs wobbled, he tucked a hand around her upper arm, holding her up with disconcerting ease. The cooler air hit her body, and her shivering started again.

After blotting her hair, he grasped her chin and tipped her face up to the light. She gazed up at his darkly tanned face, trying to summon up enough energy to pull her face away.

"No bruises. I think you were lucky." Taking the towel, he dried off her arms and hands, rubbing briskly until he appeared satisfied with the pink color. Then he did her back and shoulders. When he reached her breasts, she pushed at his hand. "I can do that." She stepped back so quickly that the room spun for a second.

"Jessica, be still." Then he ignored her sputters like she would a buzzing fly, his attentions gentle but thorough, even to lifting each breast and drying underneath.

When he toweled off her butt, she wanted to hide. If there was any part of her that should be covered, it was her hips. Overweight. *Jiggly.* He didn't seem to notice.

Then he knelt and ordered, "Spread your legs."

No way. She flushed, didn't move.

He looked up, lifted an eyebrow. And waited. Her resolve faltered beneath the steady, authoritative regard.

She slid one leg over. His towel-covered hand dried between her legs, sending a flush of embarrassment through her. The full enormity of her position swept through her: she was naked in front of a complete stranger, letting him touch her...there. Her breath stopped even as disconcerting pleasure moved through her. But she didn't know him. A tinge of fear made her stiffen.

His gaze lifted, and his eyes narrowed. "Relax, pet. Almost done." He dried then chafed the skin on her legs until she could feel the heat. "There, that should do it."

Ignoring her attempt to take the clothing, he helped her step into a long, slinky skirt that reached midcalf—at least it covered her hips—then pulled a gold-colored, stretchy tank top over her head. His muscular fingers brushed her breasts as he adjusted the fit. He studied her for a moment before smiling slowly. "The clothes suit you, Jessica, far more than your own. A shame to hide such a lovely figure."

Lovely? She knew better, but the words still gave her a glowy feeling inside. She glanced down to check for herself and frowned at the way the low-cut elastic top outlined her full breasts. She could see every little bump in her nipples. *Good grief.* She crossed her arms over her chest.

His chuckle was deep and rich. "Come, the main room is much warmer."

Wrapping an arm around her, he led her out of the bathroom, through the entry, and into a huge room crowded with people. Her eyes widened as she looked around. The club must take up the entire first floor of the house. A circular bar of darkly polished wood ruled the center of the room. Wrought iron sconces cast flickering light over tables and chairs, couches and coffee tables. Plants created small secluded areas. The right corner of the room had a dance floor where music pulsed with a throbbing beat. Farther down, parts of the wall were more brightly lit, but she couldn't see past the crowd to make out why.

Her steps slowed as she realized the club members were attired in extremely provocative clothing, from skintight leathers and latex to corsets to—*oh my*—one woman was bare from the waist up. A long chain dangled from...*clamps* on her nipples.

What in the world? Wincing, Jessica glanced up at her host. "Um, excuse me?" What was his name, anyway?

He stopped. "You may call me Sir."

Like the Marines or something? "Uh, right. Exactly what kind of club *is* this?" Over the music and murmur of voices, a woman's voice suddenly wailed in unmistakable orgasm. Heat flared in Jessica's face.

Amusement glinted in the man's dark eyes. "It's a private club, and tonight is bondage night, pet; I thought you'd have realized that from reading the rules."

Just then, a man in black leathers walked by, followed by a barefoot woman with her head down and wrists cuffed. Jessica's mouth opened, only no words emerged.

One eyebrow raised, the manager waited patiently. She could feel his hand pressed low against her back, like a brand.

What had she gotten into? "Bondage?" she managed to say. "Like men making *slaves* of women?"

"Not always. Sometimes a woman dominates the man." He nodded to the left where a man dressed in only a loincloth knelt beside a woman. The woman wore a skintight latex vest and leggings with a coiled whip attached to her belt.

"And domination can range all the way from an entire lifestyle, twenty-four/seven, to just a fun bout of sex. Many women fantasize about having a man take charge in the bedroom." He stroked a finger down her flushed cheek. "Here the fantasy is real."

Something inside her tightened at his words, a fascination mixed with shock. *Take charge*—what exactly did that mean? Then the memory swept through her of how he'd touched her naked body, how he'd simply...taken charge, and she couldn't keep from looking at him.

His dark eyes were intent on her face, as if he could read her reactions as easily as she would read a client's books. She felt telltale redness rise in her cheeks.

"Come," he said, smiling, his hand moving her forward. "Let's get something warm inside you—"

Inside her? Like the thrust of a man's—She jerked her mind away. Good grief, she'd been here five minutes, and her thoughts were in the gutter. A smart person—and she was that if nothing else— would make a polite retreat right about now.

"And then you can decide if you want to hide in the entryway or stay here with the grown-ups."

Even as her spine stiffened, she realized how easily he'd played her, and she glared at him.

His lips quirked.

As they approached the circular bar, the bartender abandoned making a drink to come over. He looked like a Great Dane with shaggy hair, all bone and muscle, even taller than...Sir. She frowned over her shoulder at the manager. What the heck kind of name was Sir?

CHAPTER TWO

"Something hot, Cullen, for Jessica. Irish coffee with lots of Irish." As Zachary gazed down at the little intruder, he had to smile. She had a lovely body with lush hips wide enough to cradle a man in softness and full breasts begging to be savored. Her skin was fair, and her eyes the color of spring leaves.

And right now, those eyes were wide as his grandmother's favorite supper plates. How she'd read the rules and not understood the nature of the club, he couldn't comprehend. He really shouldn't have let her in, signature or not, but her helplessness had brought out all his Dom instincts to protect and nurture.

"A hot drink would be wonderful," she told the bartender.

Zachary's eyes narrowed; she was still shivering a little but much improved.

The toweling off had helped, as had her dawning embarrassment when he'd handled her. Although in her mid- to late twenties, she was obviously not accustomed to being touched so intimately. Her blushes had left him with a growing desire to touch her even more thoroughly, to explore her body, and discover her responses.

But he hadn't been able to ascertain if she would welcome his attentions or not. As for if she was a sub… The votes weren't in on that yet either. However, once she moved past the initial shock of seeing the club, he'd be able to look into her mind and see if the sight of domination excited her.

The night was yet young. If he sensed desire in her thoughts, he would enjoy laying her soft, vanilla-scented body out across his bed, restraining and opening her for his pleasure.

"Master Z." One of his newer dungeon monitors stopped beside him, his bony face worried. "Could you arbitrate for a minute?"

"Certainly." Zachary glanced at Jessica. "Do you need an escort to the entry or will you be staying?"

Her mouth—pretty pink lips that would look quite lovely around his cock—pursed as she glanced around the room. He sensed her misgivings vying with her intense curiosity. The curiosity won. "I'll stay."

"Brave girl."

The creamy Irish coffee burned all the way down, starting a little fire inside her. *Heavenly.* When the bartender came back, Jessica had finished and was gazing sadly into the already empty cup.

"Ready for more?" he asked.

Heck, her purse was in the car trunk and would be there until a tow truck pulled her car out. "No, thank you. That's all right."

He leaned an enormous arm on the bar and frowned. "You obviously want another. What's the problem?"

What was it with these guys? "Are you and your boss mind readers or what?"

His laugh boomed, drowning out the music. "Master Z's the mind reader; I'm just observant."

His statement was a little too straightforward for comfort. Surely, the manager didn't read—*nah.* "I left my purse in the car, so no money."

"Not to worry. You're the owner's guest tonight." After a

minute, the bartender set a steaming mug in front of her. "There's a two-drink limit, so I made this one plain coffee."

"But I've only had one drink."

He grinned at her. "Better to have alcohol after playing, not before. Besides, you may well need more alcohol after a bit."

Now why did that sound so ominous? She sipped the drink instead of inhaling it, and this time the warmth filling her was from hot coffee and not potent alcohol. She set an elbow on the bar, sighing as the cold released its last grip. When she saw Sir again, she'd have to thank him for the drinks.

So, he was the owner of this place, not the manager. No wonder everyone jumped at his requests. Then again, she hadn't known he was the owner, and she'd let him strip her naked and that wasn't like her at all. Somehow he'd been in control from the moment he walked into the dressing room. *Master Z*, the bartender had called him; that fit all too well. She stiffened. *Bondage* club... Did that mean *he* was into tying people up?

The thought made her squirm. How could she ever face him again without turning red? She sighed, realizing she probably wouldn't see him again anyway. After all, he was way out of her class. Too good-looking. Too self-assured. With that touch of silver in his hair and laugh lines around those smoky gray eyes, he was definitely a man, nothing like the boyish types that seemed to be everywhere. And he had those lean, rippling muscles...um-hmmm.

But what really attracted her was his air of sheer competence, like whatever he did, he'd do better than anyone else. She sighed, shook her head. Duh, Jessica. A guy's nice to you, and there you go, getting all enthused.

But to her slender mother's disgust, she'd never had the trim, perky body that men liked, and Master Z would know that since he'd seen her in all her naked glory. Considering his appearance, he could have any woman in this place. Hell, any place. Yeah, she would just avoid him and not make an even bigger fool of herself.

Turning on the bar stool, she checked out the room. A *bondage* club. Now this presented her with an adventure she'd never imagined. Nothing like this existed in the tiny town where she'd grown up. And in Tampa, she'd never ventured to try anything so exotic. Shoot, her idea of adventurous was volunteering at the animal shelter.

She grinned. While here, she might as well widen her knowledge base. Aunt Eunice would be delighted, and her mother would be horrified.

But nothing thrilled her more than learning something new. Where to start?

The people dancing appeared to be having fun, although she'd never been at ease on a dance floor, at least not sober. Give her a business or social occasion, and she felt right at home. Make it a man-woman interaction, and she tensed up like a businessman being audited.

As she watched, her eyes widened. Some of the gyrating out there would have the participants arrested anywhere else. One young man with a serious hard-on whirled the woman into his arms and then pressed so close that only the fabric between them prevented insertion.

She took another sip of her drink and realized the dancers were just too provocative for comfort. Like that one couple. The man moved his woman where he wanted her. He touched her when he wanted, even put her hands on him...there.

With an effort, Jessica dragged her gaze away, tried to watch the other couples on the floor. And focused on a big man in skintight rubber jeans that bulged with a thick erection. He pulled his bikini-clad woman to him, tangled his hands in her hair and tipped her head back to take her lips. He kissed her slowly. Thoroughly.

Jessica blinked, realized she was pressing her thighs together. *Whoa, time to stop watching the live action.* Here she'd thought she could call herself fairly experienced. Sure, she was small-town raised, but she'd lived in Tampa long enough to have had several lovers. Not that she was all that good at the sex stuff. Really, making love was rather overrated, at least for her.

She grimaced, remembering the last time and how she just couldn't stop thinking about everything and anything. Did he think she was fat? Would he see how her stomach pouched out? Should she move her hips faster? Would he like his balls touched or not? Sex was just too stressful.

After finishing her coffee, she glanced back at the dance floor. Heck, that woman out there looked like she was getting more from one kiss than Jessica had ever gotten from the whole *insert-dick-move-around* shebang. And now, the man had his hand on the woman's bared breast, was actually toying with her nipple. When his fingers tightened in what looked like a painful pinch, the woman's knees sagged.

Damn, but just watching was getting Jessica overheated. Her own nipples burned. Furtively, she glanced down. No bra. Her nipples poked out like someone had glued pencil erasers to her chest. Turning back to the bar, she crossed her arms over the traitorous flesh and willed them to go down.

The bartender looked at her, a hint of amusement in his eyes. He lifted his thick eyebrows at her cup.

She shook her head. No more alcohol, and she was definitely warm enough. Time to go walk about and cool off.

Sliding from the bar stool, she headed away from the dance floor toward the rear of the room. People crowded the tables and couches; the murmur of conversation increased as she moved away from the music. The place looked almost like a normal bar if she ignored what people wore...and the hands-on stuff. She edged past a table where a woman knelt at her guy's feet. He stroked her hair like a pet cat.

Jessica frowned. The owner had called her *pet*. She did not —*really* did not—want to think about what he'd meant by that. Especially since thinking about *him* made her think of that couple on the dance floor. What would it be like if it were Sir touching her, holding her against his... *Oh, girl, do not think that way.*

Halfway down the room, she neared one of the places on the wall that was lit with brighter sconces. Now she could see what it was. She blinked in horror. There was a naked woman strapped to a wooden X on the wall. *A live woman, not a statue.* Jessica's feet didn't want to move even though she knew she was staring.

Okay, okay. This was really like a strip bar; naked women doing stuff. But the woman was *tied* there, her legs open, breasts free. Everyone could see her.

She instinctively started to go to the woman's aid, then stopped and scrutinized the people watching. No one appeared concerned. A man in shiny black latex jeans and sleeveless shirt stood within the roped-off area busy with some small metal things in his hands.

Jessica made herself study the woman on the cross thing. Eyes focused on the man in latex, the brunette wasn't hurting; her squirming movements seemed provocative.

Had that woman *wanted* to be tied and naked? Biting her lip, Jessica tried to imagine what kind of person would surrender such power to someone else, even so far as being tied up. Not someone like herself, that was for sure. She'd fought her way up the business ladder, could hold her own in social circles, was an assertive, independent woman.

So why was she finding this so fascinating?

Why did this place feel like her dreams come to life, only more erotic than anything she'd ever imagined? Her face flushed as she remembered Sir saying, *Many women fantasize about having a man take charge in the bedroom.* Surely he hadn't been able to tell that she was one of them?

She looked at the woman again. What would that be like? Heat swirled through her at the thought of being there herself, wrists lashed... *No, that was totally wrong. Keep moving.*

She threaded through the spectators, past the roped-off area.

Most of the members were in couples or groups, and Jessica felt conspicuously alone.

And underdressed, even if she wore more than a lot of the women. But her full breasts jutted out against the tight shirt, bouncing with her movements. This wasn't the sixties, for heaven's sake, and she never went without a bra. Not in public. Conservative accountants didn't wear stuff like this. Or go without panties either. The silky feeling of the skirt sliding against her bottom, the caress of cool air against her private areas was disconcerting, especially in this sex-charged room.

People brushed past, leaving perfume, cologne, and musk in their wake. A couple went by, the man leading the woman with a leash strung to a collar around her neck, and the scent of sex permeated the air around them.

Look at that. The way the man had the leash wrapped around his fist, the way the woman followed... Jessica touched her neck. Her core actually burned as shockingly wanton thoughts filled her head: a man's hands buckling a collar on her, touching her. A man —*Sir*—doing anything he wanted to her.

Across the room at the bar, Zachary smiled, enjoying the wide-eyed innocent. When she touched her neck, he hardened, knowing exactly what was in her mind. Her emotions were so strong, he could almost see as well as feel them.

"Lost your little sub, Z?" The bartender set a glass of Glenlivet down.

"Not lost. Released to explore."

She reminded him of a kitten freed from the kennel, faring forth on a new adventure, ears forward, tail held high. She was definitely a brave little ball of fluff. He had watched her stop in front of the St. Andrew's cross, felt the shock radiate from her.

Unlike most people, she had strong, clean emotions. Curiosity. Courage to explore something new. Shock. Worry and sympathy for someone she thought might be hurt. The ability to think before reacting.

And now...*arousal*. Other emotions might be more satisfying, but few were as enticing as awakening desire.

"She's a cutie," Cullen commented. "Apparently not used to seeing public displays. She was watching the dancing, especially Daniel with a sub, and she kept turning red."

Zachary sipped his drink. "Then it should be interesting when she reaches the back of the room."

Cullen laughed. "You have a twisted mind. Do you have plans for her tonight?"

"Perhaps. She's fascinated by the Dom/sub couples." Would the kitten scamper back to safety?

"Wish I could just mosey through a woman's mind like you do."

"According to the subs you've had, you do quite nicely without the talent." Smiling, Zachary turned to check the room, but the little innocent had disappeared.

This was like being Alice in a very twisted Wonderland, Jessica decided, one where all the characters had only sex on their minds. She'd been propositioned by a woman, by a fat man, by a couple trolling for a threesome. Then she'd struck up a conversation with a really cute guy, and suddenly he knelt at her feet and wanted—

"You want me to whip you?" she repeated in disbelief. Surely there were laws about whipping people?

He had big brown eyes, full lips. The chain and leather harness displayed seriously ripped muscles. He nodded vigorously. "Please, Mistress."

Jessica rolled her eyes. "Sorry, but I'm not into pushing guys around." Well, not unless they'd messed up their accounts, or forgotten to save their travel expense receipts. But order a guy around in bed? Major chill factor there, even without adding a whip into the business. *Ugh*.

He looked so disappointed, she patted him on the head before turning away. He tipped his head back to rub his cheek against her hand like an oversized cat.

This place was *so* strange.

Turning away, she continued her tour with only a touch of trepidation. After all, it couldn't get much worse than women hanging on walls, right?

Farther down, another small area was roped off, and Jessica stopped with a quick breath of astonishment. Damn, the guy had been serious about the whipping stuff. Face against the wall, a naked woman hung from shackled wrists. A short, muscular man wearing only studded black leather pants stood behind her slapping a thin cane into his open palm. Testing it. With a whooshing sound, the wooden stick smacked against the redhead's bare buttocks. The sound made Jessica cringe even before the woman's high shriek.

Jessica took a step forward, her stomach queasy. This wasn't right, shouldn't be allowed. Another step, pushing past the observers, and she'd reached the ropes defining the area. She bit her lip. *Stop and think*, she told herself.

The man had paused, and...the woman was laughing, her voice sultry, obviously more excited than hurt despite the red mark streaking her skin. Glancing back over her shoulder, the redhead wiggled her butt at the cane wielder in an invitingly lewd fashion.

All right. The woman obviously wanted to be hit. Hurt. This was way too strange; definitely not fantasy material. Jessica eyed the cane.

"Ouch," she said under her breath.

A man standing next to her smiled. His beefy build in glossy black PVC clothing made him look like a tank.

"Sounds to me like you'd like to participate," he said, his hand closing around her arm. "There's an empty St. Andrew's cross farther down."

She gasped. "No. No, I'm not—"

He dragged her away from the crowd as she tried to pry his fingers off her arm. Dammit, was she going to have to scream or something? Would anyone in this bizarre place even notice?

Screams were happening everywhere. Dear God, all sorts of bad things could happen without anyone realizing. Her hands went sweaty as fear shocked through her. Then anger hit. This was not going to happen.

Planting her feet, she hauled off and kicked him in the knee.

"Shit!" He jerked her off balance, and she landed on her knees in front of him. "Bitch, you'll regret defying me," he growled. He grabbed her hair, fingers tightening until tears filled her eyes.

CHAPTER THREE

"Let me—"

"Let her go." A figure loomed behind her assailant. The owner. Sir himself. Jessica's fists opened as relief filled her.

"Consensual is the operative word here, and she's not consenting," Sir said in that deep, smooth voice.

The jerk spun around, still holding her by the hair. "She did. You should have seen her watching the whipping. She wants it."

"Actually, she doesn't. She has no interest in being whipped and no interest in you." Sir's hand closed around the fingers wrapped in her hair, and a second later, she was free.

Her legs were shaking too badly for her to rise. Hugging herself, she huddled in place. Another man appeared, this one with a yellow badge on his leather vest. "Problems here?"

The jerk pointed at Sir. "He interrupted my scene."

"Did you just accuse Master Z of interrupting a scene?" The bouncer sounded shocked. "Master Z?"

"She's unwilling." Sir held out a hand to Jessica, and she grasped it. His hand was hard, muscular, and he pulled her to her feet so easily it was frightening. "Are you all right, little one?"

She drew in a breath and nodded. If she tried to talk, her voice would come out wussy, so she'd just keep her mouth shut.

"Come here." Master Z wrapped an arm around her, tucked her into his side. He was so big, she felt tiny next to him. Tiny, delicate. *Female.*

The jerk's grab at Jessica was intercepted by Master Z, and then the bouncer had him by the collar.

"Mark him down for a month's suspension and to repeat the entire training class if he wishes to return after that," Master Z told the bouncer. "He apparently wasn't paying attention."

"He didn't even talk to her—he doesn't—" the jerk protested.

Dragging him away, the bouncer said in an annoyed voice, "Master Z not only owns this place, asshole, but he always knows what subs want. Always."

Jessica shivered. The man had called her a sub; that would be the term then for the one being bossed around. Why was she thinking about terminology now? She managed to inhale, start breathing again. He called her a sub. There was no way that she was a sub. God, she needed to go home.

Master Z chuckled. "Rough day, huh?" He wrapped his arms around her, holding her firmly. His hand pressed her head into the hollow of his shoulder. *Comforting. Safe.*

She gave a half laugh and a shudder. "He was going to wh-whip me. And no one would have realized..." She evened her voice. "Thank you."

"My pleasure." He just stood there, holding her, letting people flow around them like water around a boulder. Unconcerned. Nothing seemed to bother this man.

"How did you know I didn't want that? Wasn't just...playing or something? You don't really...know—"

"I know, kitten." His voice rumbled through his chest as he stroked her hair. His appealing scent—light citrus mingling with a man's unique musk—made her want to burrow closer.

But she couldn't get much closer; she was plastered against

him like wallpaper. Her breasts were mashed against his hard chest, her hips cradled against his. He felt good against her. Too good, and hadn't she wanted to keep her distance from him?

His other hand was low on her back in the hollow above her buttocks. And she wasn't going all stiff at being touched. But he'd had his hands on her already, she realized, flushing as she remembered how he'd dried between her legs. She hadn't even known his name.

She still didn't know his name. She pushed herself back and looked up.

With the light behind him, his eyes were almost black as he studied her. His lips curved and a crease appeared in his cheek. "You need a drink and a chance to catch your breath." He released her from his arms and held out a hand. "Come."

Should she? She considered her options. Go with him or try to walk back through the bar on unsteady legs, getting hit on every few seconds. Well, that was easy. She put her hand in his.

Still smiling, he led her to the bar. "This time you may choose your drink."

She hesitated. *Water or alcohol?* Water would be smart, but a drink would definitely help the shakes. And somehow the fear had burned off any alcohol from before. "A margarita. Thank you."

"Cullen," Master Z said, his voice somehow carrying past all the conversations, maybe because it was so deep. The bartender glanced over.

"A margarita, please."

Ignoring the other people waiting, the bartender made her drink and set it in front of her. He smiled at her escort. "Definitely a pretty pet, Master Z."

"I'm no pet." Jessica scowled. "What kind of derogatory term is that, anyway?" She tried to slide onto the bar stool but couldn't quite manage. Wobbly legs, short—why couldn't her parents have been tall? Then she wouldn't look so much like a dumpling with feet.

Sir grasped her around the waist and set her on the seat, taking her breath away with his effortless strength and the feel of his muscular hands through the thin fabric she wore.

"Not derogatory," he said, standing close enough that their hips brushed. "It's an affectionate word for a sub."

"But I'm not a sub. I'm not into that at all. I hated what that man wanted to do. Being whipped... Just the thought makes me sick."

He tucked a strand of her hair behind her ear, his fingers leaving a tingle in their wake. "It's a rare person who would enjoy being assaulted by a stranger."

"Huh." The shakes were lessening, and her brain was starting to work again. "So a submissive person doesn't just go belly-up when some guy orders her around?"

He grinned, a flash of white teeth in a darkly tanned face. "Hardly. Just as with any relationship, a Dom/sub relationship has attraction"—he stroked a finger down her cheek and her breath stopped at the intense look in his eyes—"and trust."

Pulling her gaze from his took effort, but she managed. She wasn't comfortable at all with the way her senses had woken up, as if he'd plugged her into an electrical current. Turning, she rested her elbows on the bar top and concentrated on her drink, trying to ignore the way her body felt, the way he affected her. Hmmm, her reaction was probably from him saving her. She'd read something about that. Okay, fine.

Be cool, continue talking, girl. "What kind of trust?" His scent came to her again, appealingly male.

He curled his hands around her bare upper arms and turned her toward him. With one hand, he tilted her chin up until his gaze trapped her. "The trust that your master knows what you need and will give you what you need, even when you aren't always sure."

The words, the sheer certainty in his rich voice, sent heat

stabbing through her, a wave of need so potent she quivered inside.

As if he could see into her head, he smiled slowly and whispered, "The trust that lets a woman be tied down and spread open for her master's use."

Her mouth dropped open as she took a hard breath, the image of herself naked, spread-eagled on a bed with him looking down at her was more erotic than anything she'd felt before.

He cupped her cheek, leaned forward, his breath warm against her ear as he murmured, "And your reaction to that shows you are a submissive."

She jerked away from him, away from the heat growing inside her, and the awareness of his body so close to hers. "No way. I really am not."

Time to change the subject. She cleared her throat, her voice husky when she asked, "So, what's your name, anyway? Does everyone call you Master Z?"

He merely smiled at her and picked up the drink the bartender had left for him. His big hand engulfed the glass. When his lips touched the glass, his eyes met hers, and she could almost feel those lips closing over her mouth, over her breast... *Jeez, Jessica, get a grip.*

He set the glass down, and then, as if he'd heard her thoughts, he took her face between his hands and brought his mouth down on hers. Her heart sped up, but it was the way he held her in place that sent hunger searing through her veins. His lips were firm, knowledgeable, teasing a response from her. A stinging nip made her open her mouth, and he plunged in, his tongue stroking hers.

Everything inside her seemed to melt. A burn started between her legs, and her hands curled around his muscular forearms in an effort to keep herself upright.

With a low laugh, he took her wrists and put her arms around his neck. Nudging her legs apart, he moved between them. Hand on her bottom, he slid her closer until her mound rubbed against his thick erection, the thin material no barrier at all. When she gasped at the pleasure surging through her, he simply took the kiss deeper, his grip implacable.

By the time he pulled back, she was trembling all over; her hands dug into his wide shoulders so tightly her fingers ached. The room seemed to throb in time with her whole lower half.

His eyes crinkled when she just looked at him, unable to speak. Cupping her cheek, he sucked on her lower lip, drawing it into his mouth, his tongue sliding across it. And when he released her, a wicked smile told her that he was thinking of putting his mouth elsewhere. Her nipples tightened into hard buds.

"Master Z?" A different bouncer approached, his manner tentative. "Could you check this out? Just take a second?"

Sir's gaze kept Jessica pinned in place as his knuckles rubbed against her aching breasts. She managed to not moan, somehow, but she might as well have, considering the glint of laughter in his eyes.

"I have to attend to something," he murmured. "Will you be all right?"

She huffed out a breath. "Oh, sure."

It was good—very good—that he had to leave her; in another minute, she'd have been willing to do anything he asked, and in this place, that could be really bad. She let out a shaky breath.

His lips curved. "Don't consider yourself safe yet, pet. I'll be back soon."

Master Z—no, she wasn't going to be calling him *master* anything out loud, no matter how well he kissed—glanced at the bouncer. "Show me."

Zachary followed Matthew, one of the dungeon monitors. Not bad timing, actually. She needed time to absorb what he'd said, time to grow tantalized by the thought of being taken. She was definitely attracted, not only to the idea of domination, but to him personally. When he'd spoken of taking her for his pleasure, he'd not only felt the flare of excitement in her mind, but heard the deep breath she'd taken, seen the increasing pulse in her neck. And her reaction to a simple kiss was so heated, he'd had to control himself to not lay her out on the bar top and bring her to a screaming orgasm right then.

He couldn't remember the last time he'd been so drawn to a woman. Just watching her walk through the room with her firm stride, her chin up, he'd felt the compulsion to take her, to have her for his own.

An assertive woman. He wasn't surprised that the sub, Joey, had assumed she was a Domme. From a distance, he would have assumed the same. But up close, when he touched her, she yielded completely, even when her reaction confused her.

Everything about her appealed to him, from her lush little body to her logical mind...and the passion that kept breaking loose from her stringent control.

And she was pushing his own control to the breaking point. So, let her wander some more. Think some more. All the choices needed to be hers, right up until she handed the right to him.

Matthew stopped at one of the farther stations. A sub was tied down over a spanking bench. Her Dom had his cock shoved into her mouth, and she was crying, protesting.

"One of the observers was worried," the dungeon monitor said, "but the sub hasn't used any safe word or gesture."

Zachary tilted his head, his eyes on the sobbing woman, letting her feelings slide into him. He grinned. "It's part of the scene and her favorite activity. No worries."

Matthew clapped Zachary on the arm with a laugh. "Good enough. Damn, life is easier when you're here, boss. Sorry if I interrupted something with that little newcomer."

Biting her lip, Jessica gazed after Sir. She'd been more turned on by kissing him than by having sex with someone else. How did he do that? Affect her like that? There was something about him...not just his words...even his walk was powerful. Controlled. Back in college, she'd been to a karate exhibition where some of the black belts had that aura, an unsettling mixture of danger and discipline. She wasn't the only one who he affected, either. Club members moved out of his way; the women turned to watch after he passed.

the black belts had that aura, an unsettling mixture of danger and discipline. She wasn't the only one who he affected, either. Club members moved out of his way; the women turned to watch after he passed.

Just like her.

And he'd called her *little one*. She frowned. If another man labeled her that, she'd cut him down to size, so why had her insides melted when Sir did it? Oh, she was in deep trouble here.

After he disappeared into the crowd, she turned back to finish her drink. Trying to ignore the seductive music, she smiled at the two men who took seats beside her, exchanged introductions, and was soon in a heated conversation about tax laws.

One of the men, Gabe, had a presence about him almost like Sir. His confidence and the commanding look in his eyes gave her a funny sinking feeling inside.

The bartender's gaze had that effect on her too, she realized, as Cullen wandered back to her area. He shook his head at Gabe. "Uh-uh. Z's."

Gabe frowned. "Now there's a pity. Well, Jessica, if you ever find yourself fancy-free, I'd enjoy getting to know you better."

"I—" Unable to think of a proper rejoinder, Jessica nodded politely and watched Gabe walk away. She turned to Cullen. "What is this 'Z's' stuff? He's not my owner, dammit."

His grin flickered so quickly she almost didn't see it. "No, love, he's not. I just thought I'd save Gabe some effort. I've seen you with Master Z; Gabe doesn't stand a chance."

Jessica glared and turned her back on him. Like she was so obvious.

She wasn't, was she?

Of course not. Putting her chin up and Sir out of her mind, she smiled and opened conversations with the members around her. Strange conversations at times. One man had long chains fastened to his belt. In fishnet tops and latex shorts, two men, obviously gay—or would that be bi?—checked her out for a threesome. A woman, in skintight red latex and matching gloves to her elbows, owned a bookstore and was fun to talk with, but her heated gaze was disconcerting.

When the woman moved away, Jessica glanced around the room. Her nerves had settled. She should continue exploring since her tame world sure didn't include anything like this place. Why did she find some of this stuff so...arousing?

Uncomfortable as the admission was, she needed an answer. She'd never been one to hide her head in the sand, after all.

And this time she'd be prepared for jerks. She could also use Master Z's name as a conjuring tool: *Don't mess with me or Master Z will make you disappear.* Yeah, that might work.

Grinning, she slid off the bar stool and set out. She received two more propositions in the first twenty feet; one man was worth a second look. He had that same confidence—strength—as Master Z and Gabe. But somehow, Sir made every man in the room seem weak, unfinished. She thought of the way he looked at her—all his attention on her, not on the music or other people or planning his evening or even his next sentence. To be the focus of that intensity was heady.

And then, of course, came the question she really didn't want in her mind: *What would it be like to have all that attention on her in bed?*

She blinked and refocused her own attention to the here and now, not in visualizing Sir with his clothes off, with his big hands wrapped around her wrists and his mouth...

Argh. Stop. Look. Walk. At one of the well-lit stations, a person was tied on what must be that St. Andrew's cross the jerk had mentioned. This time the shackled person was a male whose female boss was whipping him in horrible places. Completely appalled, Jessica stared for a moment, pulling her legs together in reaction. No, she didn't want to watch this—no way. Hurrying past, she could only think, *These people are crazy.*

She passed two women talking together on a couch. The

woman in a black catsuit was telling the other, "Your safe word is banana. Can you remember—"

And what would a safe word be?

The farther she got from the entrance, the more the lighting changed, growing ominous. Ah, some of the flickering wall sconces had red-tinted bulbs.

At the end of the room, open double doors led into a wide hallway. A lot of people were milling around in there, and the noises made Jessica's stomach twist: screams, the sound of a whip, begging. Too intense. She wasn't going down that hall.

Not that she could escape all the uncomfortable sounds. As she headed toward the other side of the room, high-pitched screams rose above the hum of conversation. In a roped-off area, a burly man with tattooed arms was whipping a little brunette tied on a sawhorse-like table. The poor woman was shrieking, "Stop! Stop, please, stop!" He didn't stop. People stood outside the ropes, not doing anything. *Damn them.*

Fury seared through her like wildfire. Her sister had been beaten like that during her marriage; Jessica had suspected abuse, but hadn't acted. She would this time.

Coming up behind the man, she grabbed the whip out of his hand. "You perverted asshole, let her up, or I'll show you what it feels like!"

The man's bulldog face flushed red, and he took one step forward, then stopped, hands closing into fists at his side. Turning to a spectator, he snapped out, "Fetch me a monitor." Spinning back toward Jessica, he snatched at the whip.

Jessica punched him right in the face, knocking him down, shocking herself. Aside from karate classes in college, she'd never hit anyone. But, hey, the punch had worked.

The brief thrill disappeared as he slowly got to his feet. *Very not good.* Her mouth went dry. She backed up a step, her heart hammering against her ribs.

His eyes glinted with rage; his hand rose as he stepped forward.

"Stop." Master Z's compelling voice. The man halted, and Jessica sucked in a relieved breath. Everyone turned as Sir strode into the roped-off area. He glanced at her, then the man. "Explain, Master Smith."

"We were in the middle of a scene, and this crazy woman comes roaring out of the crowd, grabs my whip, and damned if she didn't punch me." The man rubbed his reddened chin, and his lips curved. "It's almost funny, but still, she ruined our scene."

Master's Z's gaze turned to her, and she winced at the grim look in his eyes. "Jessica, explain."

"She was screaming and yelling, 'Stop, stop,' and he kept whipping her. No one did anything." Feeling like a child called on the carpet, she held out the whip. "I took it away from him."

"What is your sub's safe word?" Sir asked the bully.

"Purple."

"Did she use it or the club safe word?"

"Nah. She wasn't anywhere close. We've been together three years, and she's only used it twice. I'm careful that way, Z."

"I know you are." Master Z turned to her, his brows together in a frown. "Did you actually read any of the rules that you signed?"

Jessica flushed, looked down. Oh God, she'd screwed up. Somehow. "Uh...no."

"I'm sorry for that. According to our rules, if you interrupt a scene, you get punished."

CHAPTER FOUR

Her mouth dropped open. Punished? "But—"

"A scene is planned in advance, Jessica, and much anticipated. Furthermore, each sub has what we call a safe word, a word to use if they get too frightened or the pain is greater than what they can stand. The safe word is never, never stop."

Jessica licked dry lips. "You're saying she didn't really want to quit? She—but look at her back; she's all red."

The people outside the rope laughed.

"If a stranger picked up a whip and struck you, yes, that would be abuse." Master Z took the whip from her hand. "However, if someone is aroused, within the context of a sexual moment, then the pain can heighten her pleasure. These two enjoy this activity. Their enjoyment —and the scene they'd planned—has been destroyed by you."

Some people like being hurt. Okay, she'd seen that already. The club had rules—rules were good—and she'd screwed up big-time in this strange world. Time to apologize, extricate herself gracefully, and retreat.

Sitting in the entry looked more and more attractive, and she was going there right now, Master Z or no Master Z.

Now released, the whipped woman joined the bully. The tiny woman's whole body trembled, and the man put an arm around her, incongruously tender, considering the way he'd wielded that whip.

Jessica sucked in a breath and looked at her. "I'm very sorry. I thought you were being hurt, and well... Please forgive me."

Master Z raised his eyebrows at the man.

"No, Z, I'm sorry. I can see she's a pet of yours, and she didn't do it on purpose, but she screwed up our scene." He kissed the top of the woman's head. "Ruined the night for us. We got club rules for this, and I want them enforced."

"It is within your rights, Master Smith, and normally, I would agree, but—"

Jessica closed her eyes. She'd not only ream out any of her clients who signed a form without reading it, but she'd also tell them they deserved the consequences. Only a person with no character—no honor—would dodge responsibility for her own actions. *Man up, Jessica.* "I did it. I'll take the punishment."

Master Z's eyes warmed in approval. "Brave Jessica." He squeezed her shoulder and then told Master Smith, "Here is my judgment. I will allow you to discipline under my control. Since she is a newcomer, the embarrassment alone will furnish the majority of the punishment. The pain intensity should not exceed a sting."

Master Smith frowned, and then his face cleared. "Guess that'll do."

Sir motioned to a barmaid and pointed to the bench where the whipping had taken place. "Clean that, please."

After fetching a spray bottle and paper towels from a tiny wall shelf, the barmaid quickly wiped down the bench.

What did he mean by pain? Jessica's gaze went from the bench to Master Z. She was getting a really bad feeling about this. "You're not going to whip me, are you?"

Smiling slightly, he drew her closer, until her back pressed against his chest. "Not a whip," he murmured into her ear.

Despite her growing fear, she could feel the hardness of his body all along hers, and it sent a shiver of excitement through her.

As he pulled Jessica's lush body tighter against him, Zachary could feel her response in both her body and mind. Anxiety, yes. But also arousal. Of course, for a submissive—even a novice—the Shadowlands would be an erotic dreamland.

And had turned into a nightmare for this sweet submissive. He should never have let her in here, and guilt carved at his gut like a dull knife. But he could make this easier for her, and perhaps even demonstrate how arousal could change the quality of pain.

Keeping her pressed against him, he nuzzled her neck, breathing in her warm vanilla scent. She shivered.

"You aren't ready for a whip," he whispered, his lips brushing her ear. "I doubt you would ever enjoy that intensity of pain." At his words, he could feel how his touch and words sent a sizzle of excitement through her to compete with her fear.

He moved his hands up to cup her breasts. If she weren't attracted to him, weren't aroused, this would be questionable behavior, but her nipples pebbled under his touch. Ignoring the crowd accumulating behind them, he focused on raising the heat in her. Her breasts were soft and heavy, and she could undoubtedly feel the warmth of his hands through the thin top.

She felt the heat of him through her shirt as his thumbs rubbed her nipples, sending blazing sensations searing through her body.

"Stop it," she hissed, squirming in his unyielding grasp. Her heart pounded with anxiety, yet she was all too aware of his hands on her, of how his larger body held her in place so easily. It was Sir who had her in his arms, Sir who made her feel safe, only there was no safety here.

She looked over her shoulder. "Wh-what are you going to do?"

"Kitten, if you find this too frightening or absolutely can't continue, you can say, 'red.'" He held her as easily as he would a puppy, his arms around her both comforting and terrifying.

Red. Like a stoplight. She relaxed slightly.

"Master Smith, could you lower the front several inches, please?" Sir said. "And bring the entire bench up another foot." Even as he spoke, he teased her breasts, rolling the nipples, stroking the undersides.

When he moved a hand down to press against her mound, a wave of pleasure rolled through her. She struggled, but she couldn't move away from his attentions, and even her fear couldn't suppress the sensations awakening in her. Or was her apprehension heightening them?

The table was adjusted.

"Jessica, bend over now," Master Z said.

Unable to help herself, she instinctively tightened her body to stay straight.

He gave a huff of laughter, moved one arm down to cross at her hips and bent with his chest against her back, forcing her down on the table. "Shhh, pet. It will be all right." Pulling her arms out to the side, he flattened her chest onto the bench.

"I-I don't—" *Don't know if I can do this.* Her hands curled into fists.

Sir straightened, and the loss of his warm body left her feeling abandoned. He moved beside her to arrange her breasts so they hung down on each side of the narrow bench top. At just his touch, more heat surged into her core.

A second later, she realized that with the bench tilted head down, her bottom was sticking high in the air. Dread scraped cold fingernails down her spine. "Sir. I'm—I don't know."

"Kitten," His hand brushed over her flushed cheek, his touch smoothing away the nerves. "This will be quick, and then you'll be done." After a light stroke down her hair, he walked over to the wall.

She twisted her head, trying to keep him in sight. Her breathing went ragged as she realized that the flickering lights on the wall had concealed what hung there. Canes and whips and paddles and crops. A whimper escaped.

She could hear people laugh. Lots of people. Watching her. A shudder ran through her.

Hands behind his back, Sir took his time contemplating the devices, and her anxiety grew with each interminable second that passed. *No, not the whip. You promised. Please, not the horrible long, stiff cane.*

He picked up a round paddle the size of a person's head. "This should fit the need."

A paddle. Surely that was better than the whip. *Right?*

He touched her cheek gently. "Jessica, since you are new to this, I will make it easy. For this period of time, you have permission to scream, to cry, to swear and call names, to beg...even to stay silent. Remember that you can say 'red' and everything stops."

Give me permission to say something? When she glared at him, amusement lit his eyes.

He disappeared behind her, and she couldn't turn her head far enough to see him. The club members ranged around the roped-off area. Spectators at a live show. Rage grew inside her at them and maybe at Master Z, as well. When someone lifted her skirt, smiles appeared.

Her teeth ground together, and an embarrassed flush seared her face. She had on no underwear; all of her butt was up and naked in the air where everyone could see.

I can do this. She forced herself not to push up. Not to run.

Sir's voice. "Such a pretty little ass, don't you think, Master Smith?"

"Very nice."

To her dismay, Master Z didn't start her punishment. Instead he massaged her buttocks. Although his hands were gentle, she

36

could feel the hardness of his fingers and palms. Not a soft man. As he ran his fingers over her bared skin, his touch grew increasingly intimate. He slowly traced the creases between her cheeks and thighs.

Her awareness filled with the bombarding sensations, the seductive assault. When his fingers stroked between her legs, sliding in the wetness there, need poured into her body like hot air through an opened window. Then he moved away, leaving her throbbing.

"As the offended parties, please take three strokes apiece," he said, his voice as courteous as if he'd been a fancy waiter.

Oh God, he was going to let *them* hit her with that paddle. Jessica shook her head, and humiliation and fear eroded her determination to stay brave. Tears filled her eyes, turning Master Z into a blur as he sank to a crouch in front of her.

"It will hurt less if you can relax."

"Please..."

"You can do this, pet. Hold onto me." After prying open her fists, he curled warm fingers around hers. He nodded at someone and *wham!*

Stinging pain burst into her right buttock, and she gasped.

Wham! Wham! As pain seared her skin, she pulled at his restraining grip. *Ow ow ow* The need to yell grew. She clenched her jaw.

And then it stopped.

Trying not to cry, she rested her forehead on the leather.

"Eyes on me, Jessica." The deep timbre of his voice was as comforting as his grip on her hands.

After a second, she rested her chin on the padded leather and looked at him.

His steady gaze appraised her for a long moment before he said, "Can you hang in there for the last three?"

No! Yet, the need to please him was compelling, and she jerked her head up far enough to nod.

"Brave Jessica."

As his thumbs stroked circles over the backs of her hands, the strangest feelings trickled through her. She could still feel the intimacy of his touch between her legs.

He looked over her shoulder at someone. "Go ahead."

She barely had time to tense.

Wham. Just one buttock. Another blow on the other. Not as hard, but the burning built quickly into pain. One final smack across both cheeks brought tears to her eyes.

"All done, kitten."

Done. Her bottom stung, but not horribly, so why did she feel like crying? "I'm s-sorry." She hated the waver in her voice. "I didn't mean to cause trouble; I didn't."

His eyes gentled to a soft gray. "I know, little one." He released her hands and rose, walking toward the end of the table out of her sight.

She laid her cheek on the leather, trying not to whimper. *No more, please, please, please.*

Something touched her bottom, and she cried out more in fear than pain.

"Pink and tender, but no need for salve." Sir's hands caressed her bottom, painful and yet almost exciting. The feeling of need edged back. "Punishment's over."

A few people in the crowd groaned in disappointment, but stopped suddenly as if their complaints had been cut off.

Master Z grasped her around the waist, lifted her to her feet, and held her steady until she found her balance.

It hadn't been that bad, so why were her insides shaking harder than her legs? She wiped her face off roughly.

"This time, deliver your apology on your knees, Jessica," Sir instructed.

Only his hand under her arm kept her from falling over as she clumsily knelt. She looked up at Master Smith and his slave. "I'm so, so sorry I interrupted. And that I didn't read the rules." Her voice quivered. *What if it wasn't good enough? What if—*

Master Smith snorted a laugh. "Sounds repentant to me, Z. Apology accepted."

"Are you satisfied, Wendy?" Master Z asked.

The short brunette nodded. "Yes, Sir." Her eyes met Jessica's with a hint of sympathy.

Jessica let her head drop forward in relief. It was over. And yet, another tear slid down her cheek. Not from pain, though her bottom still burned. But, as emptiness hollowed her chest, filling her with coldness, she had to hold in sobs. *I want to go home.*

And then Sir bent and effortlessly lifted her into his arms.

"No! Leave me alone."

"Shhh," he murmured.

As he drew her closer, pressed a kiss to the top of her head, the chill receded.

Zachary found an empty couch in the middle of the floor and settled into it, keeping Jessica firmly in his arms. Guilt was a hard lump in his guts. Never had a kind gesture gone so wrong. He should have made her stay out in the cold entry with Ben, should never have let her into the club.

Dammit, there'd been no time to arouse her enough to turn the pain to pleasure. Worse, a bare-bottom paddling could bring back painful memories of punishments received as a child.

He gentled his arms around her, settling her head against his chest. "All finished, little one."

She buried her head in his shoulder, choking back sobs in a way that broke his heart. He could feel her trying to wall up her distress, but between Dom and sub, there should be no walls. She didn't know that yet and wouldn't for a time, even if she wanted to walk this path.

True, she wasn't his sub, but he'd acted as her Dom for the punishment. Aftercare was his responsibility. This was where he would start.

He shifted her in his arms so he could tilt her head up and look into her eyes. "I have you, Jessica," he said quietly. "Let it out."

Her emerald eyes blinked at him in surprise. Had no one ever let her cry? As her tears welled anew, she shuddered with muffled sobs. Her choked words drifted to him. "In front of people... It hurt... Nobody ever..." Her barriers fell, and she cried openly, shaking as hard as when she'd been chilled from the rain.

Sensitive little one, a sheltered pet. It only made him want her the more.

He stroked her hair and told her how brave she'd been, how wonderfully she'd taken responsibility for her actions, how much he cherished her sharing with him. He praised her courage at trying to save the other sub, how rare it was to find someone willing to act to help another.

He spoke only the truth. Even though she'd been wrong to break up the scene, the bravery of her actions impressed him. More stunning had been the way she'd accepted the judgment rather than trying to blame someone else. The facets of her personality were mesmerizing, ranging from a spitfire to this yielding woman in his arms. From controlled and careful to passionately responsive. She delighted him.

Slowly, her crying turned to jerky breaths as exhaustion overcame her.

After all too short a time, he felt her mind turn on and start burying the hurt and embarrassment under layers of control.

Her body stiffened, no longer accepting his comfort. "I want to leave now."

"The rain and wind haven't lessened, and you have no car. However, you may stay in the entryway, and no one will bother you."

Her breath hissed out, and she shoved at his arms. "Let me go."

40

"We will sit here until your legs work on their own. Unless you want me to carry you across the room?"

She stopped immediately. "At least put me down."

"No."

That brought her head up, her green eyes as wet as a forest in the rain.

"I have never had to punish someone I just met," he said, letting his own anger show. "Discipline is a trust issue between a Dom and a sub. We do not have that trust between us. To have to perform a scene, a punishment scene like that, was extremely unpleasant. It bothered me to see you hurt, Jessica," he growled. "You will let me hold you and offer me some comfort in return."

Her eyes widened. Earlier, she had understood the damage her heedless actions had created with Smith and his sub. Could she grasp the discomfort she had caused him?

He could almost hear that clever mind turning over the events. This was a very smart woman.

And then she whispered, "I'm sorry" into his shirt.

"As am I," he returned evenly, not granting her the grace of forgiveness. Not just yet.

She sniffled a little, edging her way under his defenses. "What do you want me to do?"

"Just sit with me, little one, until we both recover a bit. You are a comforting armful of woman, and my body likes having you against it."

With his words, her mind opened to more than the lingering pain. He could sense the way her body suddenly became aware of him again, of his muscles against her softness, of his hand stroking her hair, of his scent. When she squirmed to ease the pain of her sore ass, his cock reacted to the provocative movements. She had the kind of body he enjoyed most: round, soft, and abundant.

As he hardened, she froze, realizing what her movements had incited.

He chuckled and pressed his lips to the top of her head. "I want a kiss, and then I'll take you to the entryway."

"That's all?" she asked suspiciously.

Narrowing his eyes, he stroked the underside of her breast, his thumb rubbing the nipple.

Her alarm was accompanied by a flare of heat.

"Maybe I should ask for more?" he murmured.

She set her hand over his, trying to pull him away, as successful as a kitten tugging on a human's hand.

"One kiss."

With an aggrieved sigh, she tilted her head up.

This time he would go more slowly. He brushed her lips teasingly, like in his days in Special Ops, scoping out the terrain. Her mouth was soft with a tiny ridge in the center of the lower lip, dividing it into two tiny bottoms. He took the kiss deeper, opening her lips with his own, coaxing her into responding. Under his slow assault, her mouth softened, much like a woman's nipples after she'd come. Still deeper, he invaded her mouth, taking possession.

Her fingers tightened around his hand, so he tightened his fingers around her breast. A gasp. He read in her mind the complex roil of emotions of a woman with growing needs. Heat seared pathways from her breasts to her pussy, and when he sucked her tongue into his mouth, it upped the sensations in her body the way an elevator carries a person to the top.

When her appealing body quivered with hunger, he drew away slowly before he could be lured into more. A promise was a promise, and she was overwhelmed already. If the chill of the entryway cooled her lust, then so be it. Of course, if her needs and thoughts drove her back into his territory... Well, his imagination had already placed her in his bed, her pussy open to his tongue, his fingers, and then his cock. He would enjoy taking her over and over until her screams of ecstasy left her limp and ready to take again.

42

He shook his head to ease down a little, then brushed another kiss over the mouth that was almost as sumptuous as her breasts.

"Up, little one." He pushed her to her feet, wrapped an arm around her as her knees buckled. Just to annoy her, to put strength back into her legs—and to see if the punishment was turning to something else—he ran his hand down her ass, squeezed each sweet cheek in turn, remembering the vivid pink that had glowed on her fair skin.

She caught her breath, and, oh, yes, another gratifying increase of heat.

"As I said, pain is a sensation very close to excitement," he murmured, still stroking her buttocks, enjoying her confusion as the soreness twisted into erotic sensation. "If I bit you there, you'd probably come."

Her back stiffened, and she tried to move away. She wasn't used to words tantalizing her desires even as his fingers did her ass.

Without saying more, although he was already thinking of what he'd be saying soon to her, what he'd say when her first wrist was shackled to his bed, he led her out to the entryway where Ben ruled in the cold and barren room.

CHAPTER FIVE

The troll guarding the door glanced up as they entered. Sir kissed Jessica's fingertips, nipped one sharply enough to send heat into her fingers and even deeper, and left without speaking.

"Got yourself kicked out?" Ben set down his pen and pushed his papers to one side.

"I didn't want to be in there anymore." Jessica settled onto the floor in the corner farthest from the door and shifted uncomfortably. Hardwood floor, sore butt...bad combination.

They'd hit her with a paddle.

The memory of the pain entwined with the memory of Master Z's hands stroking over her bare bottom, how his fingers had touched her breasts so gently. Her hands closed into fists. What kind of person was she to be aroused by that?

"Do you do that sort of stuff?" she asked Ben, jerking her head toward the door. Not that she really wanted to talk, but her mind kept shifting to uncomfortable places, much as her butt was doing. Trying to take her mind off both, she started finger combing through the tangles in her hair.

"Nope. I'm straight vanilla sex, as they call it. Z prefers that for his guards. We don't get diverted." He fumbled in his pocket, tossed her a comb.

"Thanks." She grabbed a lock of hair to work on. "It doesn't bother you what they do in there?"

He shrugged. "World's full of variety, why not sex? Everything in there is—what's the phrase?—safe, sane, and consensual. Yeah. If they like a little more kink to get their rocks off, it's no business of mine." He grinned, rubbed his jaw. "My brother-in-law is from New Orleans. Doesn't like bland food. If it doesn't bite back, he'll dump pepper sauce on it. Nice guy; just has different taste buds than me."

As he turned back to his paperwork, she stared down at her hands. Different tastes. Did she have different tastes? *Surely not.*

Those people on the dance floor—the ones who had excited her—had been the two couples where the men were obviously in charge. Sir had used a word for that, but she couldn't remember what he'd said.

"What are the terms for a guy in charge and a woman obeying?" she blurted out, and reddened when his eyebrows lifted.

"You're thinking of a Dominant/submissive relationship? Dom/sub. If the dominant is a man, he'll usually be referred to as Master or Sir or anything else he chooses." Ben's lips curled up. "His sub sure isn't going to contradict him, right?"

The smack of the paddle rang in her ears. "Uh, no. Where does *slave* come into it?"

"More often that's a person in a life relationship, where the Dom has even more control. There's some couples here like that, but for lots of people it's only for sex or playtime."

"So every night this place is filled with..."

"BDSMers? Nah. Saturdays only. Fridays are for the swinging crowd, Thursdays are leatherboys. Sometimes he'll rent the room out for private parties."

"Busy place." Master Z, they called him. So he was a dominant, and he treated her like a submissive. *Submitting to a man.*

Even as she rejected the whole idea, her body thrilled at the thought. Dammit, he'd let her be paddled until she'd been crying all over the place. Then he had held her as tenderly as a child while she cried on him.

She shifted again, trying to find some position where her butt didn't hurt. Like that would happen. So would she prefer sex to have a bite? Should she be analyzing this like she would some client's books?

Why shouldn't she take the time to study it?

Okay, then, admit it... Watching the Dom/sub couples had made her hot. Hotter than she'd felt even watching porn on TV with Matt, her last boyfriend. He'd been trying to get her more interested in sex, but the porn had been not only boring, but a turn-off.

Watching that Dom kiss his sub—no, *take* a kiss, allowing no refusal—had been far more erotic than watching a penis pumping into a woman on film. And the way Master Z kissed... Her insides melted at the memory. She shook her head. Thinking about his demanding mouth, those firm lips, would turn her brain to mush. *Think, Jessica.*

But this BDSM stuff was way over the top, wasn't it? She didn't need something kinky to get off. Sex was pleasant enough, really it was. Once she got started. And she got off at least half the time. Her orgasms were nice.

She bit her lip. Why did she get the feeling that if she went to bed with Master Z, *nice* wouldn't be the operative word? Because he'd *take* her, not have sex with her. She doubted she'd have any choice in how it would happen or what he'd do.

Just the thought of that sent moisture trickling between her legs. *Oh, God.*

Still drawing the comb through her hair, she realized the strands were free of knots, flowing down to the middle of her back. Now what was she going to do to keep herself diverted? She could hear the people inside the club laughing, talking. The music thrummed with a compelling beat.

She wanted to go back in there. Find out what she was missing. And she was too scared to do it. He'd punished her. Her ass still hurt, dammit.

A part of her brain pointed out that she'd broken the rules, and he hadn't been happy at all about having to enforce the rules.

Nonetheless, what if she went back and he did something horrible to her?

She didn't even know him.

"Is he a good boss?" she asked, her voice barely over a whisper.

"Got it bad, don't you?" Ben shook his head. "Okay, here's the rundown on Master Z. Been here for years. The club is his hobby. Nothing unlawful, no drugs allowed. Pays his employees on time. Expects his people to be professional. Divorced once, two grown children, not serious with anyone now. Women fall all over him, and in his world, he's known as the best master around. And that's according to the subs, who would definitely know." He gave her a challenging grin. "That what you wanted to hear?"

She flushed and nodded, looking down at her hands.

"Oh, and he doesn't go for the hard-core S/M stuff, whips and beatings and blood. If you're hankering after that, he's not your man."

"But—" *The paddle.*

"Not to say if a sub stepped out of line, she wouldn't get punished," he added. "But there's a difference between a spanking kind of thing and getting whipped. Or so I've been told."

"Oh."

Sir was interested in her. She'd seen that, felt his erection pushing against her. He'd be willing to take her to bed. Show her...*things.* The thought made her insides quiver, and her core throb.

If she stayed here in the entryway and left in the morning, this Dom/sub stuff would be an itch at the edge of her mind, be whispering to her every time she went to bed with someone. She'd be comparing a *what might have been* with normal sex and never know if reality would have lived up to her imagination. After all, maybe sex with a master would be just another fizzle like so much of her sex life had been.

Could she stand not knowing?

Before she'd really decided—had she decided?—she was on her feet.

"Going back in?"

She set the comb down on his desk. "Don't tell me. I'm dumber than I look, right?"

He grinned. "Braver at least."

Zachary felt her before he saw her, a compelling mix of desire, fear, and determination, and his own emotions flared up with pleasure. Although he'd hoped, he hadn't really expected her to return, not after such a harsh introduction to the lifestyle. He'd considered joining her in the entry, talking more with her, but had refrained. She should make her decisions without his influence.

Wasn't it ironic that he'd discover an intriguing woman, one where the chemistry between them was like gasoline and fire, and she wouldn't be part of the scene?

But here she was now, resolve and courage uppermost in her emotional fields. She might be innocent as far as alternative sex, but she had an admirable ability to honestly acknowledge her own needs. And the guts to go after what she wanted.

Pity her bravery had brought her to this scene, he thought, trying not to smile as she walked up beside him and froze. A pretty sub with bright red hair was tied to a spanking horse. The angle had been tilted so her ass was high in the air...much like Jessica's had been, Zachary remembered with enjoyment.

He glanced down, seeing Jessica's eyes widen, feeling her

shock at seeing the tied sub. Her imagination was undoubtedly putting her there in the sub's place, with him behind her.

The Dom in the scene squirted some lube onto his fingers and now slid two fingers into his sub's perky little asshole. The redhead wailed and squirmed—more from arousal than pain, Zachary knew. But Jessica tightened against his side, so he leaned down.

"These two have a long relationship," he whispered. "He has taken her this way over and over, and she comes screaming every time. They're both enjoying the show they're putting on, Jessica."

She was stiff until his words sank in, then relaxed. "You're sure?"

"As sure about them as I'm sure that you're not ready to have my fingers sliding into anything except your pussy."

Her sharp inhalation, followed by an intriguing wave of heat, hardened him like a rock. Yes, the attraction was definitely there. Would the trust that was needed follow?

So when she turned her face up to scold him for his bluntness, he simply took her lips, those soft pink lips he'd been craving since the last time. His arm around her foiled her attempt to step back. He set his other hand along her jaw, keeping her tilted at the right angle to toy with her mouth, to nibble on her succulent lips, to run his tongue across the velvety skin and tease until she opened for him, letting him in deeper to discover the secrets inside. When he sucked on her tongue, she melted.

Her lips seemed to burn under his as he tantalized them both until she flattened her curvy body against him in an effort to get closer. Pleasure indeed.

Reluctantly, he pulled back, taking her arms and setting her away from him. As she blinked, returned to her surroundings, the tied-down sub in front of them received her master's cock with a shriek of delight and then spasmed into a loud and happy orgasm.

Jessica turned a dark red, choked a little. "Ah. Guess you were right about them, huh?"

Grinning, Zachary put an arm around her, steering her away.

They weren't returning to the bar; he was taking her toward the front of the room. Jessica dragged her feet. "Where are we—"

"You've had a long day and probably missed supper," Sir said. "You must be starving by now."

Food? That seemed so...mundane in this exotic place, but the thought set her stomach to growling. "I guess I am."

She hadn't noticed before, since it had been on the other side of the bar, but the front corner opposite the dance floor held long tables filled with finger foods. Sir handed her a small plate, and she moved down the table, picking up tiny meat pastries, stuffed mushroom caps, crab canapés. He didn't take anything to eat, just poured them each some iced tea.

"Aren't you hungry?" she asked.

"I ate earlier."

In an unoccupied sitting area, she sat on the couch, and he took a chair. He rarely wasn't touching her, she realized, looking over the coffee table at him and feeling more than physical distance growing between them. She set the plate on the coffee table, increasingly self-conscious.

"So," she said. She was back to feeling awkward in a man's presence; wasn't that weird? "How did you come to own a club like this?"

He leaned back in the chair, obviously at ease, his legs stretched out in front of him. One lean hand held his glass of tea as he contemplated her for a moment. "The lifestyle can be a lonely one, and people turn to the clubs for company. I didn't like the abuse occurring in some of them and wanted to see if I could do better."

She started to pick up a pastry and stopped. How could she eat in front of him? He probably thought she was way too big as it was. When she looked down, her hips and thighs seemed like they bulged beneath the skimpy skirt. She folded her hands in her lap.

Conversation. They were having a conversation. "Abuse?"

"As with any alternate lifestyle, BDSM can attract unstable personalities. Here, at least, I try to ensure that consensual is more than a catchphrase. But even with screening and training procedures, we still have some problems." His narrowed gaze flickered from the plate to her hands. With a frown, he set his tea down on the table. "Are you no longer hungry?"

She shrugged, feeling gawky and inept. Why couldn't she be all slim and everything, and why did her big butt never bother her unless she was attracted to a man?

He shook his head and smoothly changed seats, joining her on the couch. "Come here, pet." With an unyielding grip, he slid her over until her thighs and shoulders rubbed his.

Could he feel the way her hips squished?

"Jessica, in case you haven't noticed, I like your body,." He gripped her shoulder, pushing her against the back of the couch, then trailed his fingers down her neck, across her breasts, her stomach.

Heat flowed into her like a current. She moved uncomfortably when his hand settled on her pudgy thigh.

"I like round." He held her gaze with his own as his hand stroked her hip. "I like abundance." His hand moved to cup her breast, and he smiled as the weight settled into his palm. And then he slid her skirt up, and his fingers wrapped around her thigh, moving upward until she squeaked and closed her legs against him.

He bit her earlobe, a tiny jolt of pain, and whispered, "I fully intend to bury myself—very, very deep—in all your softness until you're squirming under me. Until you're panting for release."

God, she was panting now, and the whole world seemed to have caught fire.

Ever so slowly, his hand stroked down her leg, and then he sat back, leaving her feeling flushed and needy. He didn't put her skirt back, she noticed.

Picking up a mushroom cap, he held it to her lips. "Eat, Jessica," he said. "You'll need your strength for later."

When her mouth dropped open at the tantalizing threat, he popped the morsel into her mouth. One warm arm around her shoulders, he continued to feed her, bite by bite, talking in his deep voice about the different people in the club. Cullen, who was a Dom as she'd thought and who went through the subs like wildfire, never taking one for more than a couple of nights. Daniel, who hadn't been happy since losing his wife three years past, also liked curvy women. Adrienne, a sub, who'd disobey just to get a whipping. Cody wanted to be a twenty-four/seven slave, and Joey was searching for a mistress.

When the food was gone, Sir smiled down at her. "Feeling better?"

She was, amazingly enough. "Yes. Thank you," she said, meaning more than just the food. She felt comfortable and settled.

"Good. Now tell me why you think your body is unattractive?"

And just like that, she was off base again. Huffing out a breath, she pretended to watch two people walking past. "I don't know where you got that—"

He cupped a hand on her cheek and forced her to meet his gaze. "Don't evade the question, pet. Was it your parents? Men?"

Why did she feel even more naked now than when he'd dried her off in the bathroom? She didn't need to talk about this with him—with him of all people.

He waited. Damn him.

"Mom, at times. And there were some men who liked their women to be thin." She shrugged, tried to look away. His hand didn't move. As his thumb stroked her lower lip, he could probably feel it quiver, dammit.

"Well-meaning parents can mess up a person's head, true. And men like that? They should pick skinny women and leave the soft, round ones for men who can appreciate them." He shook his head in disgust. "Sometimes I think our country is filled with idiots."

He really did like her body. The thought was heady. Freeing. "You're a nice man," she said.

"Of course I am." His eyes crinkled, and she saw the glimmer of a smile that reminded her of who had fondled her bare butt, had swung a paddle against that same bare butt. His smile widened.

"Ah, right." She rose to her feet, relieved when he didn't stop her. "How about you point me toward the facilities."

When he stood, looking down at her, she felt like that kitten he kept calling her. A kitten next to a wolf that wasn't hungry... right this minute. But danger was there, glinting in those dark gray eyes. She watched him warily as he set his hand low on her back then deliberately stroked the curves of her butt.

She frowned at him.

Before she could even react, he yanked her up against his chest. His hand behind her back held her pinned as his other hand roamed over her bottom—her still tender bottom—so intimately she was embarrassed and aroused all at once.

"First lesson, little sub," he said very softly. "Frowning at your Dom can be risky." One finger traced the crack between her buttocks through the silky skirt material, and she quivered under his touch.

"You're not my—" The carnal look in his eyes froze her tongue. "Um. Right. A lesson. Thanks."

He chuckled and released her, the lack of his warm body against hers like a sudden chill.

Shaking her head, she headed for the bathroom, striving for dignity but moving a little too fast to accomplish the effect. She glanced back before going through the door. A man was talking to Sir, but Sir's gaze was on her, a faint smile on his lips.

The sensual flush ran through her right down to her toes.

CHAPTER SIX

Zachary listened to James and his ideas for a scene with his fairly new sub, but his mind was more on Jessica than the conversation. He could tell her thoughts were on him and the way he'd made her feel. She was confused...and very aroused. Excellent.

He turned his attention to James, replayed mentally what the young man had said. New sub, inhibited. Wonderful in private but he couldn't get her off during public scenes.

"Then don't do them," Zachary said. His college-age son would have added a *duh* at the end.

"But I love scening in the club, Z. It's something I don't want to give up. Hell, she may not work out for me after all." James sighed, his unhappiness clear.

Zachary put thoughts of Jessica away so he could focus on the problem. James and Brandy were good together, each meeting the other's needs. It would be a shame for something so minor to cause a division. "You can scene without her reaching climax."

"Yeah, but like that's the whole point of a session, at least it is for me."

"All right then." Zachary frowned. "If Brandy comes easily

54

when alone with you, then she's inhibited by being on display. If you can bring her to orgasm once or twice in a public scene, she might well be fine after that."

"Yeah, that's what I think. She kind of likes doing stuff in front of people...just not getting off."

"A woman is at her most vulnerable then, both physically and emotionally." Zachary glanced at the restroom door. Jessica should be out soon. "James, let me give you a few tips and—"

"Shit, Z, I'm not good with remembering instructions. Can you show me? Do one of your scene lessons?"

Education was a priority at the club, and although inducing a public climax wasn't part of the usual training, it was probably a concern to many of the newer Doms and subs. "All right. Next week."

"Cool. I'll make sure I've got the night off." James's grin showed his relief before he nodded toward the restroom. "You know, I've seen your sub before. She visits the animal shelter every week."

James was a vet tech, Zachary remembered. "Doing what?"

"Socializes the animals; you know, walks the dogs, snuggles with the cats. The animals adore her."

"Good to know." A sweetheart, like he'd thought.

"Yeah, thought I'd mention it. She's not the type to boast."

"No." The woman had depths he hadn't explored yet, physically or emotionally.

"Well, thanks for the help, Z," James said. "I'm going to go tell Brandy about next week."

Right after the younger man left, Jessica returned.

Zachary turned to Jessica, savoring her straightforward emotions after the noisy jangle of the young man's. Her mind was so clear; he occasionally could get images rather than just emotions.

Right now, her barriers were back up, her arousal down. She was like hot springs on a high mountain, all that heat covered over with new-fallen snow. Now how long could she make that last, he wondered, amused. "Let's head toward the other side of the room."

The intent look Sir had just given Jessica unsettled her.

In the restroom, she'd had a firm talk with herself as she cooled. She wouldn't make an idiot of herself by getting all hot and bothered. Sure, she wanted to discover more about the bondage stuff, but not to the point of relinquishing all control. "What's on the other side?"

"Just a place to sit more comfortably," Sir said easily. "You have a soft voice, and it's hard to hear you when we're close to the dance floor."

He guided her toward an area filled with small groups of chairs and couches. People were sitting and talking quietly. Well, some of them. They passed a couch where a woman knelt at a man's feet openly playing with his cock.

Jessica turned her eyes away and blushed. "People sure aren't modest here, are they?" she muttered.

His chuckle sent tingles through her. Hell, no matter what he did, she got tingles, as if every skin cell on her body had been sensitized to his touch or voice. Just the feel of his hand stroking her bare arm made her toes curl.

Finding an empty couch, he took a seat and pulled her down beside him. He was so close that his scent wrapped around her as his weight tilted her into him. She clasped her hands together in her lap. "Now what?" she asked in a bright voice.

"Now we get serious." His dark, rich baritone made her stomach quiver. "Why did you come back in?"

The unexpectedness of the question made her insides tighten. Why did he keep asking her these impossible probing questions, dammit? How could she possibly answer this? "I didn't come for... I was just curious." Curious to see what he could do to her. Her breath quickened.

"Curious to *see*? Or curious *to do*?" He laid one big hand over both of hers.

"Mostly to see." Really.

"No curiosity as to what being restrained *feels* like?"

She grimaced. "I don't think so."

"Well, kitten, let's find out." With one hand, he gripped her wrists, pinning her hands on her lap as he cupped her cheek with his other hand.

He kissed her. When his tongue rubbed against hers, warmth filled her. She tried to bring her hands up to touch him only she couldn't, and surprise, then heat, ran through her. His mouth moved down the side of her neck, teeth closing gently on the skin, giving her goose bumps.

Again she tried to move. Again his fingers held her in place, and she actually felt herself dampen.

"You have soft skin that begs to be touched," he whispered, licking the hollow in her collarbone. "Nipples that want to be sucked." With his free hand, he ran his finger across the top of her low-cut shirt, stroking the top of her breasts.

She held her breath, wanting him to go further. Not wanting him to. Dammit, she didn't like being so confused.

Smiling, he pushed the elastic top lower until her breasts were half out. His fingertips slid under the shirt to touch one nipple, and it beaded into hardness. Her mouth closed against a sigh, and then she froze as she realized he wasn't looking down, but studying her face, her expressions. As his gaze captured hers, his fingers lightly circled her nipple, around and around, until she could feel need growing inside her, until she was biting her lip. Too many sensations: his hard hand restraining her, his fingers on her body. Urgency filled her as her core throbbed.

"Feels different, doesn't it?" he whispered. ""Do you want more?"

"No." He saw her too clearly, and that was as frightening as how her body was reacting. "No, I don't."

His jaw tightened. "I really do know when you lie, little one. For your comfort, I haven't called you on it before, but now..." His steady gaze pinned her in place. "Now you will be honest with me."

"I—" She shook her head, unwilling to expose her need. Realizing she couldn't lie.

"I think we'll go and satisfy some of your curiosity and some of that need you don't want to admit to." He gave her a level look. "Your answer is 'yes, Sir.'"

Her heart was hammering like she'd been running for miles, and her hands grew sweaty in his grasp. *Do this? Let him...do what he wanted to her?* It was why she'd returned, but the idea was insane. Yet the thought of his hands on her, taking her... She couldn't answer, could only gaze at him helplessly.

He smiled, pulled her to her feet, and led her past the bar, raising a hand at the bartender.

"Got it," Cullen said.

Sir opened a locked door marked *Private* and guided her into a small room down a hall. With a wave of his hand by the door frame, two wall sconces glowed with soft, flickering lights.

She halted just inside the door, one wrist still in his grip. The throbbing music from the club was a soft murmur in her ears as she looked around. The dark-paneled room held a massive wrought iron bed with a shimmering sapphire cover, an antique armoire, and nothing else. She licked her lips. What was she doing? This was too much, too irrevocable. She pulled against his grip.

"No, Jessica," he murmured. "You're here because you want to be. If you leave, you'll always wonder what could have been."

How did he know that?

Her breath came hard as he led her to the bed, but he simply sat on the edge and pulled her onto his lap, clasping her hand. "First of all, this time between us is simply for pleasure. Trust me to know how to give you that pleasure. Can

58

you do that?" His eyes were intent as if he could see into her soul.

She nodded then stiffened. "You won't whip me...or anything, right?"

"No, kitten." He stroked a finger down her cheek. "You've experienced the worst of the physical punishments I hand out."

Her muscles relaxed slightly. "Okay."

"Second. If you become too frightened or are somehow in pain, your safe word is red. If you use that word, everything stops. It's the equivalent of calling nine-one-one, so don't use it lightly."

A way out. That was good. She realized her hands were cold within his warm grasp.

"But, Jessica." He tipped her chin up to pin her with a hard gray stare. "If you're hurting or frightened, simply tell me." His lips curled up. "If I'm doing my job, I will know; nonetheless, I expect you to share what you feel with me."

Bare her thoughts, her emotions? Could even sex with him be as intimate? Both would leave her vulnerable... This really wasn't a good idea, was it? "Sir, I think—"

"You think too much sometimes," he murmured, releasing her hands to tangle his fingers in her hair. "This is enjoyment, not a college exam." Tilting her head back, his mouth closed on hers in a tender kiss. He kissed her slowly, thoroughly, as if he had all the time in the world. Her skin heated and suddenly she was ready to feel his hands on her, wanted his hands on her. Her fingers curled in his silky hair, and she kissed him back until her head spun.

She hardly noticed when he rose to his feet, his mouth still on hers, when he pulled her to her feet. He stepped back, leaving her out of breath, her lips tingling.

His eyes were dark, his mouth in a firm line as he turned her to face the bed. Bending her forward, he set her hands on the cool silk cover.

"Don't move your hands from where I put them," he said. "Do you understand?"

Oh... It was starting. Her heart gave a hard thud. As her fingers curled the quilt into bunches, she nodded.

"Say, 'Yes, Sir,' so I know you are hearing me."

"Yes, Sir," she whispered, and shivered.

"Very nice." He stroked her cheek. Then she felt his hands on her waist, undoing her skirt. His fingers were firm, sure. When her skirt pooled around her feet, leaving her bare from the waist down, she jerked and started to stand.

"Stay in place, little one." His hand pressed on her back, unmoving until she resumed her position, hands braced on the bed. And then he touched her, massaging her sore buttocks, murmuring in pleasure. "You have a beautiful ass, Jessica. Just right for my hands."

His fingers slid down the crack between her cheeks, touched her folds so intimately that she gasped. "You're wet for me already," he rumbled. He slid his fingers through her wetness over and over until her slit was on fire and her hips squirmed uncontrollably. But she managed to keep her hands still.

"You didn't move. Good girl," he said, and the approval in his voice filled her with pleasure.

"Turn around now." He helped her stand and smoothly pulled her shirt over her head, leaving her completely naked. "Ah, you are a beautiful woman, Jessica," he said, his eyes heating as he took his time looking her over, his gaze as warm as his hands had been.

He really did act like she was pretty. She could listen to that all night.

His warm hands ran up her arms. "Your skin is like expensive velvet, kitten," he murmured before stroking across her collarbone. Her nipples tightened even before he touched them and stroked them with his fingertips into aching need.

"Up on the bed now," he said, his voice deep, smooth. He pushed her ahead of him until she reached the middle. With steady hands, he rolled her onto her back; the way he handled her so easily startled her. He straddled her, one knee on each side of her waist. She stared up at him. His jaw was strong, darkly shadowed, and his firm lips curved a little in a smile.

He stroked her hair. "Do you trust me not to hurt you, Jessica?"

She nodded, and he waited until she whispered, "Yes, Sir."

"Good girl." His eyes never leaving hers, he picked up her hand and lifted it toward the head of the bed, wrapped a soft strap around it. He did the other. So quickly, so easily, and then he moved to lie beside her.

When his eyes left hers, she felt anxiety bubble up. She yanked against the straps, realizing her vulnerability. *God, what had she done?* She was naked, and he was... She didn't even know him. "No. I don't like this. Let me go."

"Jessica, look at me." He cupped her cheek in one big hand, forcing her to meet his dark gaze. His level, straight gaze. "Trust me to take care of you, kitten. Can you do that?"

Her panic receded a little, even more when he brushed a tender kiss across her lips, nuzzled her temple. She'd never met anyone who affected her like this. She did trust him, far more than made sense. She sighed her acceptance, stopped fighting the ties, although her body stayed rigid.

As she lay there, hands tied over her head, he stood and stripped, not hurriedly, just as efficiently as he did everything, it seemed. Oh, he was as gorgeous without clothing as she'd imagined, his skin darkly tanned, tight over the muscles beneath. Her eyes dropped lower, and she flushed. His erection was huge, thick and hard and jutting toward her, both a threat and a promise.

Following her gaze, he glanced down. "As you can see, I'm looking forward to burying myself in your slick pussy, feeling you all around me."

Her core clutched at his words, as if it had a mind of its own, heating and moistening for his invasion.

After covering himself with a condom, he joined her on the bed. Leaning on one elbow, he caressed her cheek and teased her lips in a soft kiss that quickly turned hot. His tongue took possession, smoothly plunging in and out of her mouth.

And she felt the heat returning as he toyed with her mouth, as his fingers traced up and down her neck, stroking across the tops of her breasts.

Then his hand moved down. "You are like a Christmas present"—his voice was smooth and dark—"gifting me with such tempting pleasures. Your breasts are lovely." He lifted each one, evidently savoring the weight in his hand, running his fingers on the underside, circling each breast until the nipples contracted into hard buds, aching to be touched.

She arched, trying to get closer, and he chuckled.

His fingers closed on her right breast, running over the tiny areola pebbles until they tightened even further. When he drew her nipple into his mouth, his hot, wet tongue drew shudders from her as it circled the peak. His teeth closed and nipped. She gasped. The feeling was just short of pain, sending pleasure jolting down through her like an electric line to her core.

She tried to bring her hands down, wanting to touch him, but the restraints held her tightly. She realized again that she couldn't move; she couldn't stop him from taking anything he wanted. Her breath hitched even as her excitement rose another level.

He moved to the other breast while his fingers kept playing with the first. He took her into his mouth, sucking hard until the nipple stood erect and a dusky red.

"Very pretty," he murmured in approval, and slid down. His mouth pressed against her stomach, nibbling and kissing until she squirmed under his touch, her heart pounding faster with every inch.

He knelt between her legs now, looking at her...her pussy. She flushed. Why hadn't he darkened the room? Sex was one thing; being looked at was another. That area should be private.

Tilting his head, he ran his finger down her stomach to the top of her cleft, and she caught her breath and yanked at her bonds.

He eyed her, pushed her leg out a little. Feeling exposed and vulnerable before his gaze, she resisted, unable to help herself.

"I don't think you're going to obey me easily," he mused. "You're too shy."

She had a feeling she knew what was coming. Now he'd restrain her legs. She'd heard about being spread-eagled, legs tied toward the corners. Her breath sped up even as she tried to tell herself it would be fun. At least she knew what was coming.

His eyes crinkled as he smiled at her. "Perhaps not the spread-eagle, then."

Reaching under the mattress, he pulled out a wide strap that was attached to the side of the bed. After wrapping the soft velvet-covered fabric just above her knee, he bent her leg up toward her chest, then out, and pulled the rope tight.

"Hey." Her eyes widened even as he did the same to her other leg and this time she tried to resist, but he was finished before she recovered from the shock. Rather than her legs being straight, he'd pulled her knees up toward her stomach, and outward, tipping her pussy up in the air.

"Now you are open to me," he said, gazing straight into her eyes. "Open for whatever my mouth or cock wants from you." Excruciatingly slowly, he slid his finger down between her folds, taking her wetness and spreading it. "This pretty little pussy is mine to use."

Staring at him, she shivered as her mind went blank. She was bound and more helpless than she could ever have imagined. Her legs jerked uselessly, unable to close, to move. Her usual worries about what to touch, how to move... All decisions had been taken away from her; he made them all. And arousal settled like a warm hand over her whole lower half, and dampness trickled between her legs, revealing her desire to his knowing gaze.

His warm hands ran up and down her legs, massaging the undersides of her restrained thighs. When he stroked the tender crease between her leg and pubis, she shivered. Her core coiled tighter. Leaning forward, he nibbled on her stomach, his breath warm against her skin.

When his fingers barely caressed her clitoris, need exploded within her. She quivered, her entire core burning almost painfully.

"Please," she whispered, not really sure what she wanted.

He raised his head, frowning. "Who?"

"S-sir, please." She needed more, needed something so badly she ached, her insides throbbing, wanting.

"Ah, I like *please*." His big hands curled around her thighs, holding her as tightly as the straps, and his head dipped. His tongue licked into her, and she cried out in surprise, the slick curl of him too quickly gone. But then his tongue found her clit, moving over and around in teasing little flicks, so that her breath almost stopped with each tiny touch. She needed to arch her hips, to press against him, and she couldn't move. She was open and immobile to his touch.

Suddenly he slid a finger between her swollen folds, and into her.

"Ah, ah!" Her tissues were so sensitive, he felt huge inside her. Hot. Her legs shook, straining against the straps.

In, out, one finger, then two, and then his mouth settled on her clit. His tongue stroked, soft then hard, never the same, until every nerve in her body was waiting for the next slide of his finger, the next touch of his tongue. She panted in little hard breaths.

And then, his mouth closed over her clit, and he sucked hard even as he plunged his fingers in and out of her. She screamed as electric spasms shot through her with the brilliance of fireworks. Her insides convulsed around his invading fingers, her hips jerking uncontrollably.

She could still hear her wails echoing in the room when she opened her eyes and realized he'd moved up to lie beside her. His gaze was steady on her face.

"Oh..." she whispered, astonished with herself at her response.

Nothing had ever felt like that before, as different from her little pleasant orgasms as an afternoon shower was to a tropical storm.

Her hands were still restrained, and she wanted to move, touch him. She pulled at the wrist straps. "Let me go," she demanded.

He gave her a slow smile. "Soon, little one. But I find I like your hips in this position." He moved on top of her and reached down to touch her pussy. She trembled as his skillful fingers teased her clit, her labia. "You're so very open."

He ran his cock up and down her wetness, setting off little spasms inside her. Staring into her eyes, he thrust slowly, firmly into her, hard and hot and thick, filling her completely. More than completely, deeper than was comfortable in this strange position. She struggled for breath, trying to escape, to move away.

CHAPTER SEVEN

Zachary's balls thudded against the little sub's buttocks, a tiny enjoyable jolt, as he sheathed himself to the hilt. She was slick and hot and tight around him. From her body and mind, he could sense her discomfort at his size, and he stopped to give her time to adjust. Her full breasts brushed against his chest, and he leaned down to nibble on one. He doubted he'd ever get his fill of her breasts.

Her pussy contracted around him as he sucked on one succulent nipple then the other, playing with each until he could feel her body responding, wanting more.

He gave her more. Her hips were tilted forward, and he adjusted his movements so each stroke, each exquisite slide into her body, brushed against her clit. Within a minute, she was trembling under him; another minute and she moaned, low and deep, her green eyes blind with passion.

She had so much passion that she'd kept hidden away, and the pleasure of bringing it forth was heady. Ah, but she had more to give. He continued pumping, hard and controlled. With one hand, he released her arms from the bonds. Satisfaction filled him when she grabbed him like a drowning swimmer.

She slid her hands over his back, then her fingers dug into his biceps as he increased the pace and force of his thrusts.

Her breathing was fast and shallow, broken with tiny whimpers, the pleasing sounds of submission. She was very close. He reached down and slid a finger up and over her clit.

Her scream filled the room as her snug pussy spasmed around him.

He let himself go and each intensely satisfying jerk from his cock set her off again and again. Finally spent, he laid his forehead against hers, a little shocked at how overpowering his release had been.

After sucking in a deep breath, he pushed himself up. She didn't move. Her heart was pounding so hard that her breasts shook with each beat. He released her knees, chuckled as her legs slid down, the muscles gone limp.

Rolling to the side, he stayed inside her, savoring the small twitches of her pussy around him. He snuggled her closer, soft and fragrant in his arms. Affection and something more filled him. He couldn't think of when he'd enjoyed sex more or when he'd been so attracted to a woman.

When her breathing slowed, when he could feel her emotions begin to swirl around in her mind, he asked softly, "What did you think of being tied, being opened for my pleasure?"

Her shock at his question, that he would speak of such things, made him hide his grin in her hair. That innocence was such a contrast to her sharp mind, just as her modesty hid the fiery passion beneath. The mixture enchanted him.

"I...hmmm. It's very unusual."

"When was the last time you came screaming?" he whispered.

Jessica gulped. His hand had been stroking her breast gently, like he enjoyed the feel of her skin, and she'd felt well cherished until he asked those questions. Did he actually expect her emotions to be as open to him as her body had just been? She buried her face against his chest rather than answer.

He pinched her nipple, a tiny pain, and her breath caught.

"Answer me, Jessica." His voice had chilled, and when she peeked up, his brows were together.

"Never, okay?" she muttered, annoyed with him in return. *Her orgasms were her business, not his.*

"When we come together like this, you will have no secrets from me," he said, not releasing his gaze. "You will not hide your body or your mind."

She shivered, feeling more exposed than when her butt had been in the air for all to see. His hand ran down her cheek, her neck. "You found being tied down a little scary, a lot exciting, yes?"

Eyes averted, she nodded. *Why did he ask if he knew the answers?*

He watched her for a moment, silently, long enough that she began to worry. Was he planning something else? What else could he do? She shivered as her mind conjured up horrifying... lewd...*tantalizing* images.

"And now you're beginning to wonder what else can happen in this room. In this house." His eyes held a wicked light. His mouth curved in satisfaction as her muscles tightened in apprehension and hunger.

"First, let me clean up a little," he said, and disappeared into the bathroom.

Chilled without him, she sat up, wrapping her arms around herself. Her body was well satisfied, but her emotions... She felt very confused. She had gotten what she wanted, right?

But was her response because of him and how good he was in bed? Or because she'd been tied up? How could she come to terms with her own behavior? That she'd actually let him bind her, and that she'd loved it?

Really, she should go home now, she thought miserably even as she longed to curl back into his arms.

When he came out, he shook his head. "Little sub, you're thinking and worrying again. Time to put you to work."

Work? Scrub the bathroom or—

"Kneel."

She blinked, saw the beginning of a frown on his face, and scrambled off the bed. Even as she dropped to her knees, her mind protested. She was a smart woman, a businesswoman. Surely this wasn't a position she should be in.

Her body didn't agree. She could feel her heart speeding up, her skin becoming more sensitive. Every little fiber on the plush shag rug seemed to caress her legs.

"Very nice." He stood in front of her, stroked her hair. "Take me in your mouth and suck me."

Her mouth dropped open. "But—"

"What do you say?"

He was only half-erect. "Um. Yes, Sir."

He set one finger under her chin, lifted her face. "Have you not done this before, kitten?"

"Twice. I wasn't very good at it," she admitted glumly. Her last boyfriend had been scathing in his comments over her performance with oral sex. Heck, at any type of sex.

Master Z's eyes crinkled. "Why don't you take that warm, soft mouth and put it around my cock. You start, and I'll instruct you as needed."

He liked her mouth. That was enough encouragement for her to grasp him in her fingers. His cock was soft; the head was velvety smooth as she closed her lips around it.

To her delight, he hummed in appreciation. Gently, she moved her mouth over his shaft, feeling him stiffen, elongate. The loose skin tightened around the hardness beneath, and she took her mouth away to stare. Earlier, she'd felt like he'd entered her with something huge; he had.

Chuckling, he stroked her hair again. "Continue, kitten."

At least she'd pleased him enough to get him hard. That was something, right? She slid her lips up and down, wetting him with her mouth.

"Use your tongue," he murmured. "Pretend it's my tongue on your clit. The only difference is in size."

Oooh, she remembered how his mouth had felt on her, how his ravening tongue had licked over her, around... The memory made her wet, made her clit throb. With growing understanding, she tongued the underside of his cock, toyed with the thick veins, then swirled around the head. Taking him fully into her mouth again, she sucked lightly the way he'd sucked on her clit.

His hand tightened in her hair. "Ahhh, that's perfect, Jessica. Now use your hands too."

Hands? Holding his dick with one hand, she pulled her head back and glanced up at him. He moved his legs apart, and his balls swayed, attracting her attention. She'd always wanted to touch a man there, to see what they felt like. With her free hand, she slipped her palm under one, lifting, letting her fingers caress it. So heavy and soft. But she could tell somehow, that although he enjoyed this, she wasn't driving him crazy like he'd done to her.

She really wanted to get him off.

Returning her attention to his cock, she licked her way back up, then grasped him with both hands at the thick base. She squeezed gently and muscles tightened in his legs. Yes! She took him in her mouth again, sliding him in and out, sliding her hands up and down in counterpoint. He grew harder, thicker, and her satisfaction was heady, almost as heady as the need growing between her legs, the desire to have him inside her there.

Her eager mouth was going to be the death of him. Hot and moist. Her awkward movements only made it worse, keeping his attention fully on her and what she was doing. When the urge to pound into her grew overwhelming, he set his hands on her shoulders. "You are very good at this and only going to get better. But I'm not finished taking you yet. On the bed, pet."

She gave him a final swipe with her tongue, glinted a happy smile up at him, and crawled onto the bed. Ah, the princess felt more in control now. He was delighted that her comfort level had increased.

Still, taking her in a mundane fashion wouldn't serve her well. She was a strong woman whose deepest responses apparently came when she was most vulnerable.

The armoire yielded Velcro straps and rope and another condom. He covered himself quickly. As he walked back to the bed with the restraints, he saw trepidation grow in her eyes. He could feel the hint of uncertainty in her mind. She sat with her legs tightly closed; her quickening breath jostled her breasts.

"Give me your wrists," he murmured, and waited patiently through her hesitation. He treasured the way she set her wrists into his grasp. Her trust in him had grown. "Good girl."

After smoothing the Velcro bindings around her wrists, he clipped them together and then slid a rope through the links. Picking her up, he turned her and set her onto her hands and knees. "Don't move, pet," he cautioned, caressing her breast. Her heart thudded under his fingers, the speed increasing nicely.

There was a fine line between fear that would excite and fear that would paralyze the senses. But he could feel her increasing arousal overcoming her apprehension.

He paused for a moment to stroke her hair. It was long enough to wrap around his hand, bringing other diversions to mind. The silky strands were a mixture of gold colors, slipping over her fair skin as he pushed them over one bare shoulder. He nibbled her nape, pleased to see goose bumps appear on her arms. Her body was sensitized, waiting for anything he would do.

After wrapping a wide strap around her right knee, he slipped her bound hands out from under her, leaving her balanced on one shoulder, her head turned to the side. Smiling, he tied her hands to the knee strap.

Her ass was up in the air, displaying her assets nicely. Perhaps someday they'd explore that perky little asshole. For now, he fingered the little dimples beside her spine before setting his hands on pretty cheeks that were still a little swollen from the paddling.

A shiver ran through her body.

Head down, butt in the air, unable to move.

Does this seem rather familiar? she wondered unhappily. Her hands were between her legs, tied to the inside of her right knee. She pulled at the restraints with no success, and the inability to move sent an unexpected tremor of need slicing through her. Apprehension made her heart pound in her chest as she tried to see what he was doing, what he planned. Her skin, even her core, tensed, waiting for his touch.

And then his hands closed on her bottom, and she gasped and shivered. He massaged and stroked her still-tender buttocks, where pain lingered. She shook at the feel of his fingers, the slight pain and excitement rolling together, wetting her between her legs. And she wanted more.

While one hand teased her butt, his other wakened her pussy, sliding into her juices. He ran a gentle finger through her folds and up to play with her sensitive clit. She tried to wiggle, and his hand on her butt clamped down, held her in place. "Don't move, little one."

His finger slid across her pussy, firmly, then teasing flicks, and she could feel her clit swelling.

"Your sweet little clit is just like my cock," he murmured. "Soft until stroked, and now feel how it grows harder. Bigger."

The merciless touching continued until she throbbed with the need for more. When his hand moved away, she moaned.

"I don't want to neglect this area." His sure fingers touched outside her opening then speared through the swollen inner labia into her slickness. She struggled for breath as the sensations spread from just her clit to her whole core. Everywhere he touched grew sensitive and burned with need.

She tightened around his fingers desperately, trying to hold him in as he slid his fingers in and out.

"More," she rasped.

He stopped, removed his hands from her.

Her whole pussy pulsed painfully and she whimpered.

"What do you call me?" he asked patiently.

"Sir. Sir, please touch me."

"Better." Suddenly his mouth was there, where his fingers had been. His slick, hot tongue flicked over her clit, teased her slit with swirling motions that set her to shuddering.

She panted, so close, so close, and then he moved away again, and she groaned, her hands closing into fists.

He chuckled then drove his cock deep into her in one hard surge.

She screamed as her world splintered around her, as she spasmed around his thickness, shuddering so hard her legs weakened. His hands held her in place, gripping her hips and keeping her pinned against him.

He felt even bigger in this position than the other, and now she squirmed, trying to escape. It felt like his cock had filled her completely, was up against her cervix, and she whimpered again, discomfort and desire mingling inside her.

"Shhh, just wait, little one, just wait," he murmured. When he bent over her, his cock shifted inside, driving another gasp from her. He set one muscular arm beside her shoulder to hold himself up, and his other hand played with her breasts. He rolled her nipples gently between his callused fingers until her breasts were tight and swollen, sending carnal messages to her groin.

Her hips wiggled slightly as her pussy shivered around his cock, adjusting to his size. He began to move, each slide in and out making her gasp and then moan as sensations started piling up like mountains on top of mountains. His hand was on her breast, his lips on her back. His cock inside her was big and thick. It sank between her sensitive folds so deep that his balls slapped against her pussy and sent tiny shocks through her.

Slow at first, he increased his speed from a sensuous slide to a hard, forceful pumping. She couldn't move; her hands were still restrained, and she could only take his assault. The feeling of helplessness ran through her, heightening every sensation. Her legs quivered uncontrollably; her whole body shuddered as each merciless thrust sent stabs of pleasure pouring through her body. She was so close again. Her pussy tightened around him, her hands closing into fists.

And then his fingers left her breast, and suddenly he was stroking her clit. With every thrust of his cock into her body, his finger pulsed across her tender clit, over and over.

She screamed as she came harder than before, great spasms inside shaking her like a hurricane, fire streaming through her all the way to her fingertips.

He pulled back, gripping her hips and driving into her as her womb convulsed around him.

"Kitten, you could be the death of me," he growled, and then she could feel his cock jolt as he came hard inside of her. "Thank you, little sub." He nuzzled her neck, her shoulder, before pulling gently out of her. She whined like a puppy from the shocking emptiness.

He disappeared for a second to dispose of the condom.

Eyes closed, she didn't see him, just felt his hands as he rolled her onto her side and released her restraints.

"Come here, little one," he murmured, and pulled her on top of him like a limp blanket. He took her lips in a tender kiss then settled her head into the hollow of his shoulder, and she found nothing in her to resist. His chest was damp with sweat, slick under her cheek, salty on her tongue when she gave it a lick.

Through the muscles covering his chest, she could hear his heart beating in a steady rhythm, nothing like her racing pulse.

His hands stroked her back with shocking gentleness after he'd taken her so hard. Her body felt abused, quivery. *Wonderful*.

Inside her head, she felt the same way. What was happening

to her, that a man could treat her like this and she got off on it? Got so off on it that she'd screamed and lost control completely.

She was always in control, dammit; she was an accountant.

"Being in control in bed isn't all it's cracked up to be, especially for a woman," he murmured.

She stiffened a little. *He really did read minds, didn't he?*

"Seems like the world expects you to have to do everything these days: care for yourselves, your families, your children, your jobs... Who takes care of you, Jessica?"

I do, she thought. *Just me.* But being tied up couldn't be considered being taken care of, could it? She frowned, remembering his knowledgeable hands, the way he watched her so closely, how he seemed to know exactly how to push her limits. Was that not being taken care of?

She managed to lift her head up to look at him, only to find his dark eyes studying her. And then he tangled his hands in her hair—just like that Dom on the dance floor had done to his sub—and took her mouth so sweetly, so thoroughly, it was as if she'd never been kissed before.

She was a snuggly one, he thought, listening to her mind fade away and sleep take her. She was draped across him like the softest of teddy bears, her breasts cushioned against his chest, her hips a graceful mound in the low light.

Snuggly and a screamer. Her shock at discovering how far passion could take her had been delightful, and he wanted to hear her low moans, little whimpers, and heady screams again and again. He stroked her hair, soft and silky with a little curl at the ends. Her fragrance surrounded him, a light mixture of vanilla and woman; she'd tasted like peaches on his tongue. He'd never been quite so content just to lie still and savor the afterglow.

The contentment dimmed at the thought that this might be all the time he had with her. She wouldn't be quite so complacent about what had happened here tonight once she returned to her own world.

Her world? He hadn't discovered much about her. What did she do for a living? She wasn't married or involved with someone; she had more integrity than that. Her essential honesty drew him like a moth to a bright light.

In fact, he'd found no one in a long time whose thoughts and emotions had been so engaging. Soothing. Most people were a jumble of raucous feelings, but her mind processed thoughts and feelings in a linear fashion, this emotion, then this one, each clean and simple.

Yet she was intriguing, a puzzle. The easy friendliness she showed to those around her was a decided contrast to her controlled, conservative manner. He wanted to know more.

She roused all too soon, sitting up from him and shaking her silky hair back. If she was on top when he took her, all that hair would rain down on his chest. The thought was tempting. But no, he needed to show some restraint.

He tucked a hand under his head, watching her. She was so graceful and round, and her breasts swayed gently, tantalizingly. He couldn't resist and ran his knuckles along the undersides, circled her nipples with one finger, enjoying the puckering.

"I think... Is it getting close to morning?" Her voice was husky, a little rough, and he smiled, remembering how she'd panted as her climax neared. How she'd screamed.

"It's past dawn, yes."

"I need to... I'm sure it's time to go."

Ah, reality had indeed arrived.

Someone had actually washed and dried her clothing. How many people did Sir have working here?

Being back in her conservative blouse and slacks seemed to make the evening less real. The club room was quiet now with no music, no people remaining except the bartender.

He nodded at Sir and smiled at her. A nice smile, but she still flushed. Her lips were swollen, her face beard-scratched, her hair tangled. She must look very well used.

After a moment, she smiled back. *Well satisfied.*

Master Z, with one arm firmly around her, looked at Cullen. "Still here?"

"Ah yeah. Sam got talked into doing some bullwhip lessons, and every masochist in the place lined up, hoping to get picked as a subject." Cullen grinned. "That ran really late, then as I was closing up, I found someone to play with. Just sent her home a few minutes ago."

Sir frowned. "You're missing sleep."

"Better a brunette than nightmares. I'll catch up tonight." Cullen shrugged. "Should be done cleaning up in about fifteen minutes."

"How late is it?" Jessica asked.

"Not late, pet." The bartender chuckled. "Early. It's almost eight o'clock in the morning."

She blinked. "I definitely need to get going."

"Of course," Master Z murmured.

Odd how she almost had wanted him to protest. "May I use your phone?"

"No need. I had a tow truck called. And your ride should be here."

After the dim bar, the bright morning light shocked her eyes. In the lingering winds from the storm, low clouds scudded across the deep blue sky. The palm trees lining the long drive swayed while fronds and debris skidded along the blacktop. The air was clear with a salty lash from the nearby gulf, and Jessica inhaled a deep breath before turning to Master Z.

What was the protocol for saying good-bye to someone who'd tied you up? Who'd made you scream as you orgasmed? "Um."

His eyes danced with humor at her awkwardness. Damn him, he was as cool and impeccable as at the beginning of the night.

Only the rougher beard growth marred his sleek appearance. He looked like a dangerous pirate dressed for an evening out in London.

She knew damn well she didn't look as good.

"Thank you for rescuing me last night," she said. "And for... Well..." She flushed.

One eyebrow rose and he stepped closer and pressed a kiss to her palm. "For baring your ass and paddling it?" he asked. "For tying you down and enjoying your body and making you come over and over?"

From the searing heat in her cheeks, she knew she'd flushed. Even more disconcerting, her body responded to his words, moistening as warmth pooled in her core. God, she wanted him again.

And he knew, dammit. "It was my pleasure, little one."

He laced his fingers into her hair and took her mouth, his kiss long and lingering with a new hint of tenderness. She sighed when he pulled back.

"Are you going to give me your phone number?" he asked gently, studying her, his eyes steel gray in the morning sun.

"It's—" She stopped. Did she want to continue this? Be the sort of person who did stuff like this? The night was over, and in the light of day, somehow she wasn't comfortable with the idea, even though, just gazing at Master Z, she wanted to drag him back into that little room. And do more...stuff. "I—"

His smile was faint. "I understand. Perhaps it is good you have time to think. I fear you had a rather abrupt introduction to the lifestyle."

Guilt crawled through her at the darkening of his gaze, almost as if she'd hurt him, but surely not. Ben said he had women everywhere, all he wanted. "I don't..." She trailed off, unsure what there was to say.

"I hope you come back, Jessica," he murmured. "You will always be welcome here." He brushed a kiss across her cheek, then turned and reentered the house, making her think of a king entering his castle.

Leaving her with a sense of loss deep in her stomach.

Okay. Get it together. She turned, searching for the tow truck and saw only a limousine in the driveway. Where—

"Miss Jessica?" The uniformed chauffeur stood beside the car.

A limo for her? All the way back to Tampa? Was Sir crazy? She glanced back at the front door, thought about protesting. She knew she wouldn't win, and she didn't really want to. "I'm Jessica."

CHAPTER EIGHT

The following week was fairly normal for Jessica: meetings with clients, working on the computer, wading through poorly kept records and ledgers. But something inside her had changed and apparently was as obvious on the outside as on the inside.

"You look...different," one of her colleagues said when she saw him in the coffee room.

She glanced down at herself. Same old tailored slacks and shirt. Hair in a French braid. Discreet makeup.

"No, not the clothes," he said, frowning. "Just, different. Hey, why don't you join me for a drink after work?"

Too weird. They'd dated briefly and had boring sex. He'd dumped her, which hurt her pride more than anything else. He *was* the office hunk, after all. Now his interest had returned?

"Thanks, but no. I'm pretty busy these days," she said.

"Oh. Okay." Confusion, then shock crossed his face at the refusal.

She was a little shocked too, for she had no interest in dating him again. In all reality, next to Master Z, he seemed insipid. Hollow like a Subway sandwich without any meat inside.

Pining after Master Z was not good.

At night, her tiny apartment felt more lonely than normal as she thought about the difference in her, unsure what it meant. On the plus side of the ledger, she now knew her sex drive was alive and well, that she could have fantastic orgasms just like other women. That change was so new, so mind-altering, she couldn't quite encompass it. She felt...sexy.

But on the minus side... *Well.* Leaning back on the couch, she stared up at the ceiling. Those miraculous orgasms were from being tied up, having a man tell her what to do, and making her do it. Even as she shook her head in disbelief, her body heated, moistened. Ready for more. Wanting more.

Surely she didn't want more bondage stuff. But the thought of never having sex like that again was...was like imagining life without chocolate. She rested her head in her hands.

What was she going to do?

Saturday arrived after seven days of confusion and six nights of erotic dreams. She'd fall asleep, and Master Z would be there, his firm hands holding her in place, his mouth on hers, on her breasts, on everywhere. She'd awaken, panting and aroused, still feeling restraints around her wrists, hearing his low whisper in her ears.

In her spare time, she hit the Internet, researching BDSM. What she discovered hadn't made her any more comfortable.

Now she paced across her living room. Time to decide what to do. Tonight was bondage night. She could return to the club... Or not.

This was just so complicated. She'd insulted him by refusing to give him her number. He'd had her car towed and repaired as if it was nothing. He had subs who adored him. He'd hit her with a paddle and let other people do it too. He'd given her the best sex of her life and made her feel beautiful.

He probably wouldn't even remember her name.

That thought stopped her halfway across the room. What if

he looked at her like she were...nobody. Another customer. A one-night stand inconveniently showing up. Her arms chilled, and her stomach felt like she'd swallowed cold oatmeal. Could she bear that?

She shook her head. *No. No, she really couldn't*. All her arguments disappeared in the face of such humiliation. She couldn't go back; he wouldn't—

Her doorbell rang and she frowned. At seven o'clock on a Saturday night, who could be at her door? A pizza delivery to the wrong address?

She checked the peephole—a delivery man—and opened the door. "Yes?"

"Miss Jessica Randall?"

"That's me."

He handed her a soft package. "Have a nice evening, ma'am." He left before she could respond.

Too bizarre. She hadn't ordered anything. After locking the door, she set the package on the glass coffee table and started ripping. Inside the envelope, soft tissue paper wrapped around a... nightie? Taken aback, she held it up. Definitely a nightie in a baby-doll style. A soft pink with a halter top and lacy handkerchief hem. Real silk.

She had never worn anything like that in her life. *What in the—* A card lay in the bottom of the package. Bold black handwriting. *Tonight is lingerie night for the subs. I would like to see you in this and nothing else. Master Z.*

Oh. My. God. Her heart seemed to stutter even as her legs turned wobbly. She dropped onto the couch. He wanted to see her. A thrill ran through her.

And then she frowned. She hadn't given him her number, let alone her address. How had he known where to send anything? Of course. The limousine driver, she'd given him her address. Sneaky, Master Z.

Once again, he'd known how she felt. Some men might have

shown up on her doorstep. Her heart gave a hard thud at the thought of seeing Sir. But he wasn't that pushy. Instead, he'd found a smooth way to let her know he wanted to see her. A warm feeling grew in her chest. He hadn't forgotten her.

Now it was up to her.

She scowled down at his gift. *Wear that skimpy thing?* Absolutely not.

She stared at it longer. Then, biting her lip, she stripped and slipped on the top. Cool silk drifted around her body. The halter top lifted her breasts up until they almost overflowed, and the bottom... Well, she'd seen shorter. *Really.* But not much. Although the points of the handkerchief hem dropped in front and back to midthigh, the sides only reached her hips.

She discovered a tiny G-string left in the package and dangled it from one finger. *Wear this? What would be the point?*

She walked over to a mirror. The nightie really did look pretty good on her, didn't it? She twirled so the hemline flirted with her legs. There were less modest outfits at wedding showers. He hadn't sent something that made her look totally slutty.

Actually, she couldn't imagine Master Z sending anything vulgar.

She turned again. If she left her hair down, it would cover up a lot of the cleavage. For the drive, she could wear a coat and leave it in the tiny coatroom. Her hands started to sweat.

Was she really, really considering this?

Zachary wandered through the club, nodding to the regulars. The place was filling up nicely. Lingerie nights were popular, both with the experienced and the newer crowd. He inspected the theme rooms in the back: the hard-core dungeon, the medical room, the office, the playroom. All were clean and stocked. The dungeon monitors assigned to each area were at their places.

He wondered what Jessica was doing about now. Staring in shock at his gift? Trying to decide what to do? Her confidence in herself and her attractiveness wasn't strong; that might influence her decision. Was she knowledgeable enough about her desires to set her feet on this path?

Clasping his hands behind his back, he strolled back to the main room. *How brave was she?*

———————

Stomach aflutter with anticipation, Jessica stepped into the entry of the Shadowlands.

Ben glanced up from his paperwork, and a big smile split his heavy features. "Well now, look who's back."

The welcome was sincere, and she smiled at him in return. "Guess so."

"Master Z will be pleased." He flipped through his file box, pulled out the papers bearing her signature. "The boss said, 'This time, read them.'"

She laughed and started perusing the three pages. Several times she stopped to catch her breath at the ways she could have gotten in trouble and the penalties involved. Sir hadn't lied to her about the punishment for messing up someone's scene either. If anything, she'd gotten off lightly.

Ben was grinning by the time she finished. "A little overwhelming?"

"A lot overwhelming," she muttered. If she'd read the forms last week, she'd never have set a foot inside. At least this time she had the benefit of some Internet research.

"Give me your coat, and leave your shoes in a cubby." He nodded at the built-in shoe storage beside the coatrack.

After tucking her shoes away, she took off her coat, feeling like she was stripping.

He gave a low whistle, making her blush. "You look really nice. Go on in now."

The club room was more familiar this time, although the crowd's attire had changed. The female subs were all in lingerie with the males in low-riding bottoms. The Dom types wore dress slacks and shirts, leather or latex. Her nightie was actually one of the more discreet ones. *Thank you, Sir.*

Although most of the members were in couples or small groups, there were singles also. And as she sidled up to the bar, she noticed the interested looks men—and women—cast her way. She noticed her breasts wobble under the sheer silk. Good grief, this was like being naked.

She glanced at an empty St. Andrew's cross and winced. Or maybe not.

The bartender was another familiar face. *Cullen.* He certainly hadn't grown any shorter; the man positively loomed over the customers. She settled herself onto a bar stool and winced as her all-too-exposed butt hit the chilled wood.

Cullen leaned an elbow on the bar to smile down into her eyes. "Little Jessica. I'm very happy to see you again. What can I get you?"

"I'll have a margarita, please."

When he set the drink in front of her, she realized she'd left her wallet in the coat pocket. "My money's in the coatroom. I'll be back in—"

He shook his head. "Nope. Didn't make that clear last time, did I? This is a private club; the members' dues cover their drinks. And you're Master Z's guest."

"That was last time. This time—"

"He's expecting you, sweetie. This time, too." His grin was slow and appreciative as he studied her. She flushed. "He also said if you were brave enough, you'd be a treat for the eyes. As always, he was right."

She actually felt a quiver inside at the appreciation in his eyes.

CHERISE SINCLAIR

Glancing away, she realized the tall man next to her was ogling her breasts. With a huff of exasperation and embarrassment, she turned toward the dance floor. Her eyes widened. Leathers and lingerie certainly made for...interesting dancing. The chemises, baby-dolls, and nightgowns offered very little protection against a Dom's hands.

Wetting her lips, she looked away and tried to see if Master Z was around. But what could she say to him anyway? *Hi there, want to tie me up again?* Oh, God, she shouldn't have come. This was too awkward, too embarrassing. She started to slide off the bar stool.

Hard hands grasped her around the waist and set her on her feet.

"Jessica, I am pleased." Sir's voice, deep and dark and smooth, sent a thrill running through her from her head to her toes.

She looked up into his intent eyes, then away, unable to meet his gaze. Chuckling, he held her out at arm's length and studied her. He smiled. "Quite as lovely as I had imagined. The pink suits you."

"Um." He wore a black silk shirt again with some of the buttons open, revealing his corded neck and hard upper chest muscles. She had run her hands over that chest, played with the springy black hair. Her fingers tingled; she wanted to touch him again. Wanted to *be* touched.

"Thank you for the...for the gown," she said awkwardly. The all-too-thin fabric offered no barrier to the heat and strength of his hands.

He rumbled a laugh. "The gown was for *my* pleasure, pet." Pulling her into his arms, he took her mouth in a lingering kiss. When he lifted his head—when her head stopped spinning—she realized he had one arm curved around her waist, and his free hand was rubbing her thong-bared buttocks.

She stiffened, tried to pull away. His grip tightened, tilting her hips into his. Fully erect, he pressed against her pubic area in a way that made her catch her breath.

"I look forward to taking you tonight," he whispered in her ear, "to hearing you whimper and scream as you come."

Heat shot through her so suddenly, so fiercely, she almost staggered. With a deep laugh, he released her and set her glass in her hand.

Cullen had been watching. Now he grinned at Sir. "Feel free to share your pet anytime."

To Jessica's alarm, rather than laughing and saying "no way," Master Z inclined his head. "I'll keep that in mind."

Her mouth dropped open. He wouldn't... They didn't... Relief filled her as Master Z curved an arm around her and headed toward the rear of the club.

After a few feet, he stopped. "I almost forgot the rest of your clothing."

From the glint in his eyes, she didn't think he was talking about a concealing robe. "What would that be?"

He held one big hand out. "Give me a wrist."

Oh, God. Asking for a wrist meant restraints, didn't it? A tremor rushed through her and she felt herself dampen. "Now?"

"The only acceptable response from you is 'yes, Sir.'"

She swallowed hard. "Yes, Sir." Even as she placed her left wrist into his hand, warmth pooled inside her.

He unclipped something from his belt, and her eyes widened. How had she missed seeing what he carried? One side of his mouth curved up as he buckled a suede-lined leather handcuff snugly around her wrist.

"Next one."

It was harder to give him her hand this time, knowing what he had in mind. But she did.

With an approving smile, he put the other cuff on her.

She turned her hands over and studied the cuffs. Sturdy leather. The right cuff had one metal ring; the other cuff had another ring hanging from the first.

His intent gaze captured hers and didn't move away as he

snapped the rings on the two cuffs together, binding her hands together in front of her. This wasn't in private. She pulled at the cuffs, her breathing increasing when nothing gave. "I don't think I like—"

"Actually, you do," he said, running the knuckles of one hand over her breasts where her nipples had tightened into hard points. When she tried to step back, he merely tucked his fingers around where the cuffs joined and held her in place.

She shook her head as he continued touching her, stroking her breasts.

"What are you feeling now, Jessica?" he asked, as if he wasn't rolling one nipple between his fingers.

"I—noth—" She stopped. *No lies*, he'd said. But...

"Just stop and think about your body, little one. Are you excited?"

Her heart beat quickly. Her breasts seemed to have swelled under his hands. Her private areas were wet and throbbing.

People walked around them; she could hear soft chuckles, but couldn't look away from Sir's intense eyes.

"Answer me, kitten. Do the cuffs excite you?"

"Yes." She felt like such a slut. Kinky sex, that was all she wanted.

He smiled slowly, his gaze heating as he leisurely looked her over. "I like seeing you in them." He touched her neck. "And seeing how they made your heart speed up." He ran one hard finger across her lower lip. "How your lips tremble."

He reached under her skirt and touched her so intimately, she choked. He lifted his fingers to his face, then hers. She could smell herself, so different from his scent.

"I can smell your arousal," he said.

Oh, God.

He chuckled. One hand around her waist, he strode through the crowd nonchalantly, as if he wasn't walking with a woman whose hands were buckled together in front of her. Reading about this stuff was sure a lot different from doing it.

"Where are we going?" Jessica asked, then grimaced. "Um. Am I allowed to talk?"

"Good question." He stopped, pushing her long hair back behind her shoulders. So much for her attempt to hide her cleavage. "Normally a sub would ask permission before speaking. But I want you to ask questions, so..." He ran a finger over the top of her breasts. "For tonight, you have permission to speak freely, unless I give you an order or until I take away that permission. Is that clear enough?"

"Yes, Sir."

His approving smile had the butterflies in her stomach doing loop-de-loops. "As to your first question, I try to do the rounds every hour or so," he said. "I like to keep an eye on the crowd, the activities. I don't believe you've seen the entire club yet, have you?"

"No." Jessica's gaze winced away from a man strapped to a bondage chair. A woman in a metallic blue bustier and leggings was tying ropes around the man's balls. Sweat poured down the man's face and chest.

They'd reached the double doors on the back wall. The area she'd avoided last time. Sir led her down a wide hallway where long glass windows alternated with doors on each side.

Z stopped her at the first window. "This is the office."

She wrinkled her nose in perplexity. Why would he have his office here? And why were people crowded around the window to the room? She edged forward to peek around a man's shoulder. *Oh.*

The room had a desk, rolling leather chair, books on shelves, thick dark red carpeting. Nice office. A man sat behind the desk writing while his secretary—a woman with her hair in a bun, and wearing a tight skirt and white blouse—was on her knees, sucking his cock.

CHERISE SINCLAIR

Jessica licked her lips, then whispered to Sir, "Guess it's not your office, huh."

He grinned, a white flash of teeth, then led her farther down the hall.

The next room appeared familiar, and Jessica jerked to a stop. "That's a—"

"A gynecologist's table, yes. This is the medical room."

A man, bare from the waist down, was being assisted onto the exam table by another man in a doctor's white coat. Jessica shivered, remembering the feel of a doctor's hands down there in that private place. *How could that man do that, knowing everyone could watch from the window?*

Even worse, the next room had the window glass slid open. People leaned over the windowsill, watching avidly as a man dripped hot wax onto a woman strapped to a table.

Horrified, Jessica wrenched away from Sir, backed away. Torture. That was torture, plain and simple.

Master Z held his hands out to her, gaze steady. "Jessica."

After a moment, she put her cuffed and chilled hands into his warm ones. He smiled faintly, pulled her into his arms, and held her firmly against his chest like a child.

"The lifestyle runs from a little bondage all the way to severe pain. I avoid subs who need pain like that, for I do not have a liking to dispense it. Can you trust me to know how much or how little pain you would find enjoyable?"

"No pain is enjoyable." She buried her head in his shoulder. "That's just wrong."

"And after your bottom was paddled, how did it feel?" he whispered, running his hand over her bare ass, reminding her of how the pain had mingled with excitement, making her hotter.

She couldn't answer.

He didn't make her, though his gaze was too knowing. He knew how it had made her feel. *Damn him and that mind-reading stuff.*

The next room, darkly medieval with chains dangling from a rock wall, contained only three people. A naked blonde lay face up on a roughly hewn bench, her arms and legs shackled to the floor. A woman slapped the blonde's legs with a flogger while a man sucked on her breasts. Giving thin screams, the restrained woman arched her back, pushing her breasts up.

"The dungeon," Master Z said. "It becomes more popular as the evening goes on, as does the playroom."

The last room was huge. One round high bed, at least three times the size of a king, took up almost the entire room. Five people were in there, twisting and turning in various positions, all entangled together. One woman on her knees sucked on a cock while a man pounded into her from behind. Two men...

Jessica's mouth dropped open as disbelief ran through her, then a thrill of excitement. "How...unusual," she said, her voice husky.

Standing behind her, Sir put his arms around her, one hand cupping her left breast. He kissed her neck, murmured, "Your heart just sped up. Something interest you here?"

"No. Uh-uh." She tried to take a step away from the window, but he didn't move. Holding her with an unyielding arm around her waist, his other hand slipped between her legs and under her thong to the growing wetness there. He stroked her clit with his slickened fingers, over and over, until she squirmed uncontrollably.

"I grow tired of your prevarications, pet." His voice had turned firm. "Answer me."

She tried to close her legs, but his hand was there, spreading her pubic lips open. One finger slid into her, and she jerked as warmth shot through her body. He wouldn't make her—

"I-I... Okay. It... I've never seen that."

"There's more," he growled, obviously dissatisfied with her answer. The finger pushed deeper inside her.

"Sir." She sucked in a breath and gave up. "It's exciting."

"What part did you find exciting?"

"The woman with two men," she whispered, her face flaming hot.

"Anything else?"

Her hips tilted into his hand as he kept up the slow stroking. "People watching."

"Thank you for being honest, kitten." He squeezed her in a brief hug. "I know this is hard to talk about for you. Although we've moved past the days when only the missionary position was acceptable, society still insists sex should be only one man and one woman in private. It's hard to get past that mind-set, especially for someone as conservative as you."

The matter-of-fact logic was steadying, his understanding of her personality even more so. Just then, the man in the room behind the woman shouted his release, and the woman came, her hips jerking frantically.

And Jessica could feel moisture trickle down her thigh.

"Mmm-hmm, I think you're getting past your inhibitions nicely," he said, amusement in his voice. He kissed her neck then released her, leaving her throbbing.

CHAPTER NINE

They went back to finish their drinks; then Sir ignored her protests and took her out onto the dance floor. The music was slow and romantic. She could do this, especially with Sir holding her warmly against him. He danced like everything else he did, competently with a firm lead.

"How did you get so good at everything?" she murmured, enjoying the soft music, the slow glide of his hand up and down her back. He'd unhooked her wrists, and she savored the feel of his hard shoulder muscles under her fingers.

"You haven't seen me anywhere but here, pet. Your opinion might be a little overstated."

Somehow she doubted that.

"What do you do when you're not here?" He seemed too straightforward to be a lawyer or businessman. Maybe—

"I'm a psychologist."

She jerked back, stared at him. "You?"

He burst out laughing. "That amount of amazement isn't exactly flattering."

"But—" Well, heck, no wonder he read her like a book. "Then you don't actually read minds?"

He pulled her back, nuzzling the hairs at her temple. "Within a short distance, I can actually read minds. Emotions, rather, and limited to what the person feels at that moment." His hands curled under her butt, pressing her against his cock, keeping her half-aroused with his attentions. "Since I work with young children, being able to know what they're feeling is essential."

Sir. Working with children. And she could actually see it; she'd never met anyone more comforting, more able to make a person feel safe.

Still... "I'd have figured some sort of sex therapy, considering... this." She waved her hand at the room.

"Counseling children is my gift to the world." He grinned, rubbed her against his erection until her legs felt weak. "*This* is what the world gives me."

Her body moved into aching need at the feel of him against her mound, the feel of his hands cupping her butt. How did he do this to her?

"Um—" She'd forgotten the question she'd been about to ask.

"And you, Jessica? What do you do for a living?"

Question. He'd asked her a question. "I'm an accountant."

His soft laugh ruffled her hair. "I should have known. You would be a perfect accountant."

"What does that mean?" she asked. Her hands came down from around his neck. She pushed him away enough to frown into his face and move his tormenting hands away from her butt.

He grasped her wrists and put her hands back around his neck. "Leave your hands there, pet," he ordered. And then he put his hands back, only this time he slid his hands under her skirt so he was touching her bottom.

Her feet stopped.

"If you're not dancing, my fingers can do this," he whispered, moving one hand to her front, sliding between her legs, under her G-string. She jolted as his fingers explored her folds. "Dance or enjoy?"

She set her forehead against his chest, shivered as his fingers brushed over her clit. "Dance, please."

When his chuckle rumbled through his chest, she shivered again.

After returning his hand to her butt, he resumed dancing. "As for being an accountant, you're extremely smart, logical, conservative, controlled. You like organization and facts. And, at least when it comes to man/woman relationships, you are more comfortable with numbers."

He didn't even bother to ask her if he was right. He knew he was. "Pretty boring," she muttered.

"Ah, but under all that control is a wealth of passion and a very soft heart," he whispered into her ear. "Not boring at all."

Okay... That was okay then. Satisfied, she snuggled closer into his arms.

She was just full of surprises, Zachary thought, enjoying the feel of her ass in his hands. He wouldn't have dreamed she'd have an exhibitionistic bone in her body, let alone an interest in ménage. He'd enjoy exploring those pursuits with her further.

An accountant. He smiled into her hair, no longer vanilla scented but lightly floral. No heavy perfumes for Jessica. A thought came to him, and he asked, "Do you own anything besides suits?"

She gave him a disgruntled look. "I have a couple of dresses."

He raised an eyebrow.

"Fine. Office attire. But I have jeans too."

"Now that I'd like to see." That curvy ass would look fine in tight jeans. It certainly looked fine in the negligee. The V of the skirt offered flashes of her butt, something he doubted she realized.

The music ended, and the next song started, a fast one for the younger members. Tucking an arm around her, he noticed again how nicely she fit against him.

Maybe she should have a sample of one of her new interests. "It's a nice night out; let me show you the side yard."

The grass was cool against her bare feet, the warm tropical air scented with night-blooming jasmine. Sir led her away from the door, weaving through tall bushes. Soft lights illuminated the fountains scattered here and there, leaving pools of darkness. The landscaping formed small, secluded areas where Jessica caught glimpses of bare skin in one, heard a low moan from another.

She bit her lip and glanced at Sir. This was just a tour, wasn't it? She'd been anticipating a visit to that little bedroom again; surely they'd be going back there, wouldn't they?

"Ah," Sir said in a low voice. "I think you'll like this spot." He turned into a small area, not as secluded as some, she noticed uneasily. A tiny fountain on one side gurgled like a rocky stream, glimmering with a golden light. On the other side was a long, cushioned bench... No, she realized, a swing, hanging from the huge live oak behind it.

Master Z sat down on the swing. "I'd like you on my lap, pet." And he grasped her around the waist and lifted. "Bend your knees," he said and placed her on her knees, straddling his legs.

"Relax," he murmured, waiting until she lowered her bottom onto his thighs. Smiling, he set the swing in motion then pulled her forward into a kiss.

His mouth slanted over hers, his lips firm and demanding, and she felt herself start down that slide into arousal. When his hand cupped the back of her head, holding her in place for his kiss, her insides melted like hot butter. God, he could kiss.

She would have been happy kissing forever, but she felt his hand behind her neck. Her halter top dropped away, exposing her breasts.

"Hey!" She grabbed the fabric to hold against her. "There are people out here," she whispered frantically. "Don't do that."

He sighed audibly. "Little sub, give me your wrist." He held out one hand.

"Sir." It sounded like a whine even to her. She closed her mouth against further protest and set her hand in his.

Without even looking, he snapped her wrist cuff to the wire of the swing behind his left shoulder, then did the same with her other wrist on his right. She pulled back, started to move her legs.

"No, kitten. If you move your legs, I'll strap them down."

She froze.

"Very nice. Just where I want you," he murmured, cupping her breasts in his warm hands, his thumbs rubbing her nipples.

She could feel the growing dampness between her legs. With gentle hands, he lifted her slightly higher and took one nipple in his mouth. Her fingers curled around the back of the swing as he sucked. Sensation jolted through her. She tried to listen for people coming, but his mouth was so insistent, and when his teeth closed gently on the tip, she sucked in a breath at the exquisite pain-pleasure. Her pussy had started throbbing, and she barely refrained from rubbing herself on his leg.

He lifted his head, his eyes dark in the shadows. Watching her face, he reached under her skirt to stroke between her legs. "Lift your hips up," he told her, his hand pressing upward against her mound, the pressure electrifying.

As she raised herself slightly, he tugged her G-string off one hip and moved the crotch to one side. She almost moaned when he slid his finger through her wetness and started playing with her clit. His fingers were firm, then soft, sliding up and down, and everything in her focused on that spot. And then he took a nipple into his mouth, sucking urgently, his tongue rubbing the nub against the roof of his mouth. She jerked as too many sensations flooded through her, as everything in her tightened, waiting, nearing—

When he moved his fingers, she whimpered at the loss, at the unfilled need searing through her.

"Shhh, kitten." He covered himself with a condom from his pocket. Grasping her hips, his powerful hands lifted her higher until she was balanced on her knees. He slid his hard, thick cock into her and yanked her down until he was buried inside her, filling her to bursting. Her cry shocked her and brought her back to sanity. God, there were people around.

"What if someone comes past?" she hissed, freezing, resisting his hands on her hips. People seeing them... The thought was horrifying and oddly exciting.

He leaned his head back on the swing, the set of his jaw stern. "Listen closely, pet. If you cooperate nicely, then they'll just see you sitting here. If you continue to ignore me, they'll see you naked on your back on the lawn, with your legs on my shoulders and me inside you."

The image made her shiver in embarrassment, yet sent another roll of heat through her, and he could tell.

His grin flashed. "Kitten, you never fail to surprise me," he murmured, laughter in his voice. He started to reach back for the cuffs. *He wouldn't, would he?*

She jerked upward on his cock, the feeling of his sliding within her so erotic, she moaned before whispering, "I'm sorry. Stay on the swing. Please, Sir."

He chuckled, putting his hands back on her hips. He lifted her —and this time she didn't resist—upward until his cock was almost out and then slammed her back down on him, his shaft thick within her, her pussy clenching at the sensation. Up and down, his hands hard on her hips, the pace unrelenting. Her world narrowed to the overwhelming pleasure of him moving inside her as each merciless thrust sent her closer to the edge.

Somewhere she could hear voices, knew they could hear the slap of flesh, the creak of the swing, and she shuddered. His hands tightened on her hips, not letting her slow. Moaning, she closed her fingers around the back of the swing.

And then he leaned her forward and took her nipple in his hot mouth, sucking hard. Angled forward, her next downward movement slid her sensitive, engorged clit across his hard pelvis, and with a set of screams, she broke under the waves of pleasure, bucking against him uncontrollably. Her pussy rippled and contracted around his hard length, setting off his own orgasm, and his hands dug into her hips as he ground himself against her.

Her head bowed as her body went limp. He balanced her with one hand. "Hold on, little one, while I release you."

A second later, unrestrained, she sank forward onto his chest, trembling with aftershocks. Every time the swing rocked, his cock moved inside her, and her insides convulsed again. He kissed her hair, holding her in the way she was coming to love, with his arms firm and tight around her.

"Let me up for a moment, kitten," he said eventually. After disposing of the condom in a concealed receptacle, he resettled her on his lap with her legs together on one side. The swing moved gently; they simply rocked for a while. The fountain gurgled. Footsteps and murmurs came from people walking past their secluded nook.

The air was soft on her bare shoulders, his hand warm as he stroked her breasts. Breasts—she stiffened. Her halter was still loose. Her fingers closed on the material, and then she hesitated, glancing up at him. His lips quirked, and his hand didn't move from her breast. Dammit.

"Compared to what someone saw a few minutes ago, this is nothing."

Those people—Oh God. "Why didn't you stop?" She glared at him.

He tilted her chin up. "Because you heard them too, and it only added to your climax."

With a moan, she hid her face in his shoulder. "What is wrong with me?"

"Absolutely nothing." He let her snuggle back against him. "Each person is different when it comes to exhibitionism. And you knew they'd only get a quick glimpse of what we were doing."

"What about you?" she asked after a minute.

He stroked her hair. "Oddly enough, I don't care one way or another. But a Dom's responsibilities include exploring your needs, both the desires you know about and those you haven't experienced. I think, someday, you might well enjoy being on display—"

She started to protest then remembered the naked woman on the St. Andrew's cross, up there for everyone to see, and felt the slow slide of heat through her.

Sir chuckled. "And I'd enjoy seeing you there."

That thought made her burrow closer. She listened to his heartbeat for a while, slow, even, calming. Had she ever had a man that just liked to hold her? Had she ever been content with just being held? The stillness between them was so comfortable...

Okay, one question from last week was answered. This was more than just BDSM stuff; she wanted Sir himself. She wanted his hands, callused and hard, on her body. She wanted more of his intense eyes, his deep voice, his attention.

Oh, she was in trouble now.

CHAPTER TEN

Under Sir's amused gaze, Jessica re-tied her halter. Then they wandered back out into the main room, making a slow circle of the bar. Sir knew everyone there, and Jessica couldn't help noticing all the longing looks he got from the women in negligees. The subs. Not that he seemed to notice. He kept her close, one hand always on her. Each touch moved to new areas, until her skin grew so sensitive that even the brush of his slacks against her thigh made her shiver.

"Z, I heard you'd requested a bottom for tonight." A tall man in black leather pants and vest leaned against the back of a couch, a darkly beautiful brunette curled at his feet. Jessica remembered seeing the man on the dance floor last week, kissing a different sub. He continued, "Vance is clearing the medical room for your scene."

"Ah. Would you believe I had totally forgotten about the lesson? Thank you for reminding me, Daniel." Sir glanced down. "Jessica, this is Master D. He occasionally works as a dungeon monitor here."

Was this the Daniel who had lost his wife, and who liked soft women? She realized he was gazing at her with overt appreciation.

She flushed, knowing her lips were swollen from Z's mouth, and the nightie didn't hide nearly enough of her.

"I'll be happy to watch over Jessica while you're busy, Z," Master D offered with a wicked grin.

She felt Sir's arm around her turn to iron, and his voice was icy, but quiet. "Thank you, Daniel. I don't believe I'll try your resistance in such a way."

Master D blinked, and his eyebrows rose. "Well now... I see."

"Z, my dear." Leading a collared blonde sub on a leash, a pretty woman in a red vinyl catsuit walked up to them. "We're looking forward to your scene. Did you want to use my slave or —" Her gaze ran over Jessica, and she smiled slowly. "That's a pretty morsel you have there. Will you be using her instead?"

Jessica glanced up at Sir, her stomach twisting. He wanted another woman for...for what?

"Thank you for the offer, Melissa. Give me a moment." Sir grasped Jessica's shoulders, turned her to face him. His smile had disappeared. "Little one. Last week, I promised to give a short training scene. I'll be using a sub, but... I don't think you are ready for this, kitten."

She saw the woman's slave staring at Sir with open lust, all but drooling. Jessica's hands tightened into fists. Z was *her* Dom, dammit, at least for now. And he wanted her to let him use someone else. *Put his mouth and—*"I'll be your sub."

"Jessica, you don't realize what this would entail."

Butterflies swarmed into her stomach, making her voice quiver. "It would be in public? In that medical room?"

"In that room. In public. Yes."

"Doing what?" she managed to ask. Maybe she could keep her clothes on.

"That would be up to me, pet." He stroked a finger down her cheek. "Pleasure only, no pain. But the decision is yours."

Could she stand seeing him with someone else? No. "I'll do it. Use m-me." Jessica choked a little on the last word. *Was she insane?*

"Well." He tilted her chin up, studied her face until she had to tuck her lip between her teeth to hide the trembling. "You are still very new to this. Are you certain?"

She gave a jerk of her head. *Yes.*

Zachary frowned as Jessica's feelings washed over him. Her fear was mixed with a possessiveness that pleased him immensely. And he saw that taking another sub at this point would damage her growing trust in him. But the lesson he'd promised James wouldn't be easy for her, although she was perfect for the role.

Her eyes narrowed as he considered, and he could feel her determination. Stubborn little minx. How did she get him into these situations? He sighed.

"So be it." He set an arm around Jessica's waist. "Daniel, Melissa, thank you for your offers."

Daniel grinned. "Your sub seems mighty feisty."

Melissa snorted. "That won't last long." She tugged at the blonde's leash and headed toward the back, saying, "Come, slave, I think we'll watch this."

Z pulled Jessica closer and followed. He could feel the way her legs wobbled and shook his head. He'd probably have to carry her out of the room afterward.

The hallway had filled with people. As Jessica entered the medical room, she realized the windows had been slid open so the audience could hear. They'd be listening to Sir. To her. Oh, God.

She pressed her lips together and straightened her spine. Be brave, she told herself, putting a hand on the exam table for balance. Besides the table, the room held a small sink with a cupboard above it, a metal tray table, a rolling stool, even an upright lamp. Very much like her doctor's office. And, hey, she'd survived pelvic exams before. Breast exams, vaginal exam, speculums—she could handle this.

Sir took a white lab coat from a hook on the wall and shrugged it on, transforming himself into a doctor. Looking oddly correct in the part.

A locked drawer in the cupboard yielded three packaged objects. He set them on the tray table. A speculum maybe? But what were the other two?

Touching her cheek lightly with his fingers, he gave her a warm look, then said, "Undress, please, and climb up on the table."

She glanced at all the people, her heart quailing as she realized everyone was staring at her.

Sir tilted his head at her, his eyes level. Waiting.

She'd told him she could do this; she'd insisted, and so she would.

Her fingers trembling, she undid the halter ties, sucking in a breath as her breasts were exposed. She heard whispers from the people outside the room, and her jaw tightened. She knew what they must be saying. Naked was bad enough; being fat and ugly made it all worse. Her nightie dropped to the floor.

"Stop."

Her hands froze in the process of pushing the thong down.

She realized Sir was right in front of her. He cradled her face in his hands, looking deep in her eyes. "Jessica," he murmured in a low voice the audience couldn't hear, "you are a lovely woman with a gorgeous body. Although there may be some fools who want skinny women, I don't. There are many others here who share my preference and adore your type of body."

He'd said that before, but now, with all these people, he must be ashamed of her. "Are you sure?" she whispered.

Shaking his head in obvious exasperation, he pressed her hand against him, against a rock-hard erection. "This is what seeing you naked does to me."

He liked her body. The glow of that kept her buoyed up as she removed the thong, as she climbed up onto the table. The leather was cold against her bare skin. She glanced at the people crowding the windows and then couldn't pull her gaze away.

With a huffed laugh, Master Z stepped directly in front of her, blocking her view. "Look at me—only at me," he ordered. Her eyes met his, his so very dark and gray, crinkling at her, and she felt better. A little better.

"That's right. In fact, I think we'll blot those people out altogether," he murmured. "Close your eyes."

She hesitated.

He growled, "Jessica."

She swallowed and complied. He put something soft over her eyes, tying it in back—a blindfold—and held her hands firmly when she instinctively reached up to tear it off. After a minute, she regained her control and put her hands in her lap.

"Lie down, little one," he said, moving to a position beside her. One arm behind her back and a hand between her breasts, he pressed her flat onto the table. Her legs dangled off the end. "Are you comfortable?"

No, she wasn't; oh, she really wasn't. She managed a nod.

Silence.

Moistening her lips, she whispered, "Yes, Sir."

He chuckled. "Let me rephrase that so you can be honest. Aside from being terrified and embarrassed, are you comfortable?"

The room was warm enough, the table cushioned. "Yes, Sir."

He took one of her hands, kissed the knuckles. "Very good, kitten. I'm proud of you and how brave you're being. I know this isn't easy." The enjoyment of his praise lasted only seconds, until he said, "Now, being a good doctor, I'm going to make sure you don't move."

Expecting him to put her feet into the stirrups, she was shocked when a strap was cinched across her body, just below her breasts, pinning her arms to her sides. Heart pounding, she yanked at the restraints. She couldn't move. "Sir!"

"Shhh, little one." His hands came down on her shoulders. "Nothing here will hurt you. What is your safe word?"

She could feel little quivers running up and down her whole

body as her breath came fast and shallow. He waited, his hands resting on her shoulders, the warmth, his presence so reassuring. He wouldn't hurt her. She was all right, and she was stronger than this. She couldn't back down now and disappoint him. She managed a deeper breath. "Red. It's red."

"Do you trust me?"

She gave a little nod.

His hand cupped her cheek. "Brave kitten."

"This lesson covers one way to introduce a novice to public scening," he said, his voice louder, like an instructor. "In Jessica's case, she is very new, and I'm proud to be awarded her trust. Trust or not, with a new sub, shyness can be difficult to overcome. One type of inhibition is the focus of tonight's lesson.

"We, of course, begin with a breast exam." His fingers lifted her breasts, stroking in circles, massaging. "Healthy breasts, as you can see."

Okay, she was good. She'd been expecting something like this.

His fingers found her nipples, stroked them to hard points, pinching hard enough to make her squirm, never quite hard enough to hurt.

"And sensitive also."

Each pinch woke more nerve endings in her breasts, in her core. She couldn't see him, couldn't see where his hands were, and her skin grew acutely sensitive as if anxious for the next touch of his fingers.

His hands ran down her torso, stroked her stomach. She heard him move from her side toward the end of the table, then the squeak of the rolling stool. She knew what was coming next. Her legs closed involuntarily before she forced herself to relax. A ripple of laughter came from the spectators.

"Because our little sub here is a novice, for her comfort, I will ask for quiet during the demonstration."

The noise of people dropped to whispers. Firm, warm fingers

closed around her right ankle, and he ordered, "Give me your foot, Jessica. Now."

She heaved in a breath, let him lift one leg and place her right foot into a stirrup. She gritted her teeth when a strap closed around her ankle, pinning her foot to the cold metal. Dammit, her doctor never used straps—restraints made it way more nerve-racking.

He grasped her left foot. Drawing her legs apart, he set it in the other stirrup. The air felt shockingly cool against her heated tissues. Another strap over her foot. She was restrained—arms, feet. *Blind.*

Her hands closed into fists as she tried not to panic.

And he waited, one warm hand running up and down her calf. "With new subs, the experience of being in a scene can be overwhelming. The embarrassment, even the fear, can keep them from moving into arousal or achieving release. As a result, often the regular amount of stimulation will not achieve its purpose for first-timers."

Her muscles loosened as she listened to his warm, deep voice.

Then he grasped her hips, slid her toward the end of the table. "Positioning is very important with the exam table," he said. "The patient's ass must be well over the edge." He let go.

"And with what I'll be doing, allowing too much movement wouldn't be good." Something was fastened across her lower abdomen. A strap, holding her firmly in that place.

He pushed the stirrups sideways, widening her legs until she was gaping open. *Oh, God.* She could do this. She must. Her legs were shaking uncontrollably.

Something scraped across the floor. A click. She could feel the heat of a lamp between her legs—on her private areas—and she gritted her teeth.

She heard someone move, heard Sir's voice next to her. His fingers stroked down her face, and his lips brushed over hers gently. "Easy, little one, no one will hurt you. Are you in pain?"

She managed to say, "No, Sir."

Then he said, "Start very slowly, softly," and she didn't understand what he meant until hands settled on her breasts. Not Sir's hands.

She arched in the air, shaking her head. "No."

"Jessica." Sir's voice was quiet, but firm. Implacable. "You do not have permission to speak. Can you be silent?"

Gags—she'd seen pictures on the Internet. His voice said he would do that; he didn't lie. She gave a jerky nod.

"Excellent." His steps sounded, moving toward the end of the table. "Continue, please."

The stranger's hands moved, softly stroking breasts already sensitive from Sir's attentions earlier. She tried not to pay attention, to ignore them, but the fingers were callused and excitingly rough against her tender skin. She could feel her nipples tightening in betrayal.

"Very nice," Sir murmured. "And down here, we'll start here with a surface examination. Pretty pink lips." A finger stroked down through her folds, making her jerk in shock. He touched her lower, against her rectum, and she tried to not cringe away. "Healthy little ass, never been used."

His fingers touched her core.

"Good lubrication, nice and slick," Sir announced, then gently pulled her outer lips apart, exposing her more fully. She tried to pretend it was just a regular exam. She'd had them before.

"For those who haven't had their anatomy lessons," Sir said, "this is a pretty pussy. The vagina extends upward from here." A finger stroked her folds, and then slid into her, and she gasped as heat shot through her. She couldn't be getting turned on in front of these people; she couldn't.

He removed his finger, slid back up through her folds. "And this is the clitoris, or clit, extremely sensitive. It must be kept slick with juices."

His finger swirled inside her, making her hips wiggle and then up, up onto her clit, sliding over and around until need tightened inside her.

"Nipples," he murmured, leaving her confused until the stranger's fingers circled her tight nipples, fingering each little pebble, pulling gently until her back was arching.

Sir's fingers were suddenly gone, leaving her empty and needy. "Now, let's go over some methods to overwhelm resistant subs." The sound of a package being ripped open. "I have a fondness for this little toy. Three speeds. Again, sufficient lubrication is mandatory."

A squirting sound then fingers at her asshole. She shook her head wildly, trying not to yell in horror as something was pushed up and into her rectum. Something slick and hard and foreign. This was no doctor's exam. She strained against the restraints, hands and feet. Nothing gave.

"Are you hurting, Jessica?" Sir asked, stroking her leg. Waiting for her answer.

At his calm voice, she stopped pulling at the straps, tried to think. The thing pushed up in her felt strange. Wrong. Horrible. But there was no pain. "No, Sir," she whispered.

"Honest little one," Sir murmured. She felt his fingers between her buttocks, and the thing moved within her. "I'll set this to slow."

Vibrations started in her ass, the sensation startling. Gritting her teeth, she tried to rub her bottom against the table to dislodge it, to make it stop, only her butt was too far out over the edge, and the stomach strap kept her in place.

"Then we have this little toy," Z said. Another paper-ripping sound. "Personally, I prefer quiet in the center with vibrations front and back. So rather than a vibrating dildo, I often use this. Also on slow."

Something touched her clit, settling so gently onto her that she didn't react at first. Then a tiny hum sounded, and the thing was vibrating right on top of the sensitive tissues his fingers had already aroused. Her hips jerked upward as every nerve in her body jolted into awareness. She moaned.

"Excellent." Z chuckled. The vibrations on her clit somehow made the ones in her ass even more arousing. Between the sensations, she felt his finger stroke around her pussy, teasing her until her inner leg muscles spasmed. "Mouth, please."

Suddenly a hot mouth closed on one breast, sucking her nipple up, tonguing it firmly. She arched with a cry that rang through the room.

"Finally, for the coup de grâce, you see the everyday dildo. This one is soft latex with gentle ribbing."

She felt just the touch of teeth on her nipples, the vibrations in her, on her clit. Her core tightened. She was shaking, coiled tightly, hurting, needing just that little more to send her over—only she didn't want that. Orgasming here, in this room? She didn't want to lose control in front of these people. *No, no, no.*

Panting, she started going through the multiplication tables in her mind. *Eleven times eleven is one hundred twenty-one. Concentrate, dammit.* She felt the horrible urge to climax recede.

Sir chuckled, murmured, "Well, there's a stubborn sub."

To her surprise, the vibrations stopped on her clit, stopped in her rectum. The mouth left her aching nipples, leaving them wet, the air cool.

Sir was silent; only his hand running up and down her calf let her know he was there.

Was she done? Was it over? Her head spinning, she sighed in relief, then started to worry. Sir had obviously wanted more than just a medical exam-type scene; he'd wanted her to have an orgasm. Here, in front of all these people. And now he'd be disappointed in her. The thought hurt, but she just couldn't—

Then the vibrations started up again, now hard and fast on her clit, in her ass. A hot, wet mouth closed on one nipple while fingers pinched the other. Gasping, she went rigid, shot back into shocking arousal.

And then something hard and thick slid into her vagina, engorging her as it was thrust in and out, pushing her tissues harder against the vibrations on each side. Her hips jerked uncontrollably as it slid in and out, and suddenly every sensation combined all over her body. She couldn't stop it. Bright lights exploded behind her eyes as massive spasms enveloped her. She screamed, screamed again and again, her body jerking as her vagina contracted and billowed around the hard intrusion in her body.

Everything seemed to go dark, still for a moment. Then she realized people were cheering, applauding. She gasped and jerked as the dildo was removed, leaving her empty. The vibrators had stopped; gentle hands removed them from her sensitive clit and asshole. She lay limply on the table, her heart hammering. Hands gently stroked her breasts. She could feel Sir's rough cheek against her tender inner thigh, then his lips.

"As you can see," Sir said, "the vibrators are an excellent tool for novice play; the combination of the three will compel an orgasm that a shy person would inhibit otherwise.

"And"—his fingers began to stroke her down below, one finger sliding between her swollen folds—"once that barrier is broken, the next climax is easier to induce."

The finger, two fingers, set up a hard stroking into her pussy, curling up and hitting a spot where she suddenly felt need flowing over her, her hips jerking in time.

"A woman can easily come again if you find the G-spot. And, of course, in this position, her clit is nicely available."

As the fingers inside set up an urgency, a coiling she couldn't evade, Master Z's mouth settled on her clit. His tongue ran over her; his lips closed around her as he sucked her clit into his mouth. She bucked uncontrollably against his mouth, yanking on the restraints with a high scream as he forced her into a long, hard orgasm.

He stroked her inside and out until her muscles were too weak to spasm further before withdrawing his fingers. The stool squeaked as he rose. "And that brings this lesson to a close. Come and talk with me later tonight if you have questions."

The sound of the whispers diminished until the area was quiet, and Jessica could hear her own gasping breaths.

"Easy, kitten, it's over. You'll be free in a moment."

Heart pounding, trembling all over, Jessica couldn't seem to move as Sir unfastened the straps on her feet and arms. When he pulled the blindfold off, she blinked in the light and focused on Cullen's face. *Cullen?*

"You, sweet sub, have lovely breasts," he rumbled, planting a hard kiss on her lips, and then walked out of the room.

Her shaking increased as Master Z helped her to sit up. Without speaking, he wrapped a thick, soft blanket around her, picked up her nightie, and carried her out into the noisy bar.

CHAPTER ELEVEN

Zachary found a fairly deserted corner and settled onto a couch with his shaken little sub in his lap. Club members walked past, occasionally nodding with a smile, none speaking. James gave him a grin and a thumbs-up.

Jessica still hadn't spoken when he leaned back with her huddled against his chest.

"You were wonderful," Zachary murmured, holding her firmly in his arms, letting her return to the world in her own time. "I'm very proud of you, little one."

She was shivering, a continuous trembling through her whole body, and he wrapped the blanket tightly around her, settling her more comfortably against him. He rested his cheek on top of her head, content to relax with her. For a Dom, the intense focus required for a scene, especially with someone so new, was exhausting but exhilarating at the same time.

For a sub... Forced past her inhibitions, Jessica had given freely of her responses, holding nothing back. Yet for someone with her personality—modest, controlled, reserved—to be so abandoned in front of strangers would be a shock to her very system.

If she needed to spend the rest of the night just being held, then so be it.

As her trembling slowed, she could hear a slow thudding in her ear, more real than the music playing elsewhere. The fragrance of citrusy soap mixed with a man's musky scent surrounded her, and she realized her cheek rested on skin and springy chest hair. There were arms around her.

She blinked, feeling snuggled and warm. Safe. A blanket covered her from toes to shoulders, hiding her from others. Her gaze lingered on the people walking past, people who glanced, but didn't speak.

She just lay for a time, unable to get her thoughts to gather quickly enough to want to move. She was in her *happy place*, her little nephew would have said.

Sir—and it was Sir, she recognized his scent and his arms— didn't seem to be in any hurry to leave. Eventually, she managed to pull in a deep breath and lift her head.

His hand stroked up and down her arm. "Welcome back, little one," he murmured, his voice sending a funny quivering through her. She could feel his lips touch her hair.

She pushed herself up a little, turned so she could watch him, feeling like she was seeing him for the first time. He was so...male, so in control. He had lines at the corners of his eyes; his beard-shadowed jaw was strong, his face lean and hard. Black eyebrows quirked up now as she touched his chin. When his lips curved up into that faint smile of his, she ran her finger across his lower lip, noting the velvety softness overlaying the firm. Very much like him, so smooth on the surface, but unyielding—demanding —underneath.

"I don't remember leaving that room." Her voice was hoarse, a little raw, and she frowned. "I don't remember a blanket."

He lifted his hand from her shoulder to caress her face. "When a sub experiences something so intense, it's not unusual for her to retreat inside, into her own head. We have blankets in all the rooms."

"Oh." Wow. But being held like this was wonderful. She let her mind drift back to what had happened, the helplessness, the sensations that had grown more and more overwhelming until she couldn't stop herself from coming. She remembered Cullen's hands, mouth on her. She shivered.

People watching.

She stiffened a little. "You told them how to handle a novice... How did you know I'd let you...?"

"I didn't, pet." He brushed her hair back from her face. "Both Daniel's and Melissa's subs are new to public scening."

"Oh."

Lowering her head, she whispered into his shoulder, "I was so embarrassed."

"I know." His hand cradled the back of her head; his steady heartbeat under her ear was comforting. "I could tell. You were also excited by it."

She stiffened. Surely not. All those eyes, staring at her, at her naked breasts, her... A shiver ran through her. *Damn him for knowing.* "A little, maybe."

"Mmmhmm."

"You let...let someone else touch me." The shock of that still reverberated through her.

"I did. Why do you suppose I would allow that?"

What was this, a test? But she was too comfortable, too exhausted for outrage. Why did he? "To give me more...stimulation?"

"Good." He kissed the top of her head. "That was one reason. But I might not have taken that method with a different sub. Why you?"

He had done that just for her? But... She froze as the answer came to her. "Because of the way I reacted at the playroom. The two men."

"You were aroused at the idea then. And once you moved past being horrified, you were aroused by Cullen's hands on you."

Oh, God, she had been. "Doesn't that bother you? To share?"

He huffed a laugh. "I find I am more possessive with you than normal. But what kind of a master would I be if I know you want to experience something, and I don't make it happen?"

He'd done that for *her*? She felt his arms around her as she thought about it. How it had felt when Sir's hands had been on her and another man's mouth on her breasts. A disconcerting hint of arousal unfurled inside her. She'd liked having two men. Oh, she had. How many bewildering revelations about her was Sir going to uncover?

"Am I supposed to say thank you?" she grumbled.

"Eventually, I think you will," he said, a hint of laughter in his voice.

"Why Cullen?"

"You like him, pet. Having a true stranger touch you might have been too much to deal with afterward. At this point in time."

And the unstated promise of more curled her toes and wiped out any words she could think to say.

"I was pleased you felt brave enough to volunteer, kitten. And I'm very pleased with you. You trusted me enough to let go, to take care of you; that is the building block for everything." He kissed her so gently; she felt tears in her eyes. "It's unusual for circumstances to toss a person into this so quickly. You're a strong woman."

She huffed out a breath. "I don't feel very strong right now."

"No. And that's why we will simply sit here and watch the world go by for a time."

"We've already been here quite a while," she guessed, watching his eyes for confirmation. "Shouldn't you be out and checking on things?"

He bundled her back against his chest, his voice a rumble in her ear. "You, pet, are more important than things."

And he held her.

———————

Eventually she sat up again. "I'm ready to move."

"And so you shall." He folded the blanket back from her shoulders.

Cool air brushed over her naked breasts, and she squeaked, covering herself. With a low laugh, he picked up her nightie and slid it over her head. After fastening her halter top behind her neck, he adjusted her breasts with sure hands, as if he had the right to touch her so easily.

"You're blushing again." He held a finger to her cheek, eyes narrowing. "After everything I did in the—"

She put her hand over his mouth, trying to silence him.

"My fingers were in more intimate places than your breasts," he whispered, ignoring her hand. The jerk. "As were my mouth, my lips, and my tongue."

The memory of the way she'd shattered the last time, under just his hands and mouth, sent warmth pooling back into her groin. "You are impossible."

His lips curved under her fingers. "And you were very loud."

Oh, God, she had been. She pressed her forehead into his shoulder, hiding her face. "How can I ever face anyone here again?" she moaned. "They saw—"

He took her shoulders, pressed a kiss to her cheek. "Kitten, many of the subs here have done a public scene."

"That doesn't help." Every private place on her body had been on display.

"Up we go," he said briskly, setting her on her feet. He tossed the blanket over the back of the couch. When she smoothed her too-short skirt down, she realized she wasn't wearing anything at all underneath it.

"I think you deserve a drink, don't you?" He tucked an arm around her as he strolled her to the bar. She really did love how he kept her so close to him, as if he was proud of her.

Cullen was there, and she froze, still a few feet from the bar. He'd *touched* her, sucked on her breasts. Sir's arm urged her forward, but her feet wouldn't move. She looked up at Sir, shook her head.

He sighed; his gaze met Cullen's. Cullen had been watching them. *Oh, God.*

Sir tilted his head toward her, and she tried to back away, but the grip that had been so gentle was now a steel band around her waist.

Cullen came around the bar. She stared at the floor, blinked when his big boots appeared in her field of vision. "Jessica."

She couldn't move. His laugh boomed out. A callused hand caught her chin, forced her gaze up. "Don't panic, love. Since you are Master Z's sub, I can only touch you with his permission, and I can see that won't be happening often at all. He only let me play because you needed the extra sensations to take you over the top."

And because Sir knew that she was turned on by the thought of two men. Surely Cullen wouldn't know that.

He grinned at her, a slash of white in a brawler's face. "I thoroughly enjoyed touching you, pet, but you don't need to run from me. Are we clear on that?"

She nodded, unsure why she'd been so frightened.

"If you'd permit, Z, I'd like a hug from your sub to know I'm forgiven and we're all right again." He stepped back.

Sir murmured, "Permitted," and his restraining arm dropped away.

Cullen held his arms out. Waited. His eyes had that look that Sir's got, the unspoken command.

Okay. She liked Cullen; he'd only been nice to her. And...*okay*. With a breath, she took the one step to him, felt his arms come around her, very different from Sir's, but comforting just the same. He was so tall; her head only came to the center of his chest. He squeezed her once, let her go.

"There." He stroked her cheek with a finger. "All better. Now, what can I get you to drink?"

CHAPTER TWELVE

For the next few hours, Sir didn't try to take her into any of the scene rooms or do more than fondle her and take a kiss, as if he knew she wasn't ready for anything more intimate. Not at this time. They wandered through the crowd, joined people here and there to chat, and avoided the more intimately engaged couples.

They were just like a normal couple on a date, she thought, trying to ignore the way her body felt when close to his and the way his voice could heat the air around her.

"Got a nasty problem in the dungeon, Z." One of the monitors trotted up, his face flushed.

Master Z took two steps in that direction, then stopped and frowned at Jessica.

"Mmmh, not a good place for you." He led her to a nearby sitting area occupied by a trim woman of around forty and a plump blonde about Jessica's age. "Ladies, may I leave Jessica with you?" Sir asked.

"Of course, Master Z," the older woman answered. "We'd be happy to stay with her."

"I can go with you," Jessica whispered to him.

"Not the dungeon, not if there's trouble," he said, pushing her into a chair. To her surprise, he hooked her hands together, then to a long chain on the floor, before giving her a hard kiss on the mouth. He glanced at the women. "Thank you, ladies."

They barely had a chance to smile back at him before he strode away, moving deceptively fast.

Well. Jessica yanked at the chain that was long enough for her to stand and maybe take one step. "Dammit, what did I do wrong this time?"

"You're new, aren't you?" the brunette said.

Jessica nodded.

"My name's Lenora. You didn't do anything. The chain says you've got a Dom already, that you're not available."

"Oh." As relief washed through her, Jessica leaned back in the chair, curling her feet under her. "Thank you."

The blonde leaned forward, her nightgown longer than Jessica's, but the top much tighter and lower. "I've never seen Master Z chain anyone outside of a scene before. He must really like you."

Jessica laughed. "I should be complimented by being chained? I don't think I'll ever understand this place."

"It's pretty strange at first," Lenora said. "But this is the best place in the area to learn. Master Z keeps his eye on stuff."

It was one of the things she found so admirable about him. "So, maybe you can tell me—" She glanced up as a man in fancy red leathers walked up, smiling at her.

"Hello. I haven't seen you before."

His bearing proclaimed him a Dom, but he lacked that special something that Master Z and Cullen and Daniel had. He saw the chain attached to her wrist cuffs and scowled. "Already taken, huh?"

He turned toward the little blonde. "Maxie, come with me."

Maxie shook her head. "I don't want to be with you, Nathan, and I can't leave here, anyway."

His face darkened. "I don't take back talk from subs, especially not cunts like you." He reached down and grabbed her wrist.

Jessica jumped to her feet and realized with her arms chained, a punch wouldn't go very far. She kicked the guy instead, right in the butt.

He dropped Maxie's hand and whipped around. Majorly pissed.

As he advanced, Jessica backed up until the damned chain went taut. Balancing most of her weight on one leg, she got ready to kick with the other foot.

"Stop now." Daniel strode up and yanked Nathan's arm behind him, pushing until the guy went on tiptoe to keep his shoulder from being dislocated.

Nice job, Jessica thought; he made it look so easy.

"Time to call it a night, buddy," Daniel said, his voice easy, his face angry. "Someone will be in touch about your membership." He hauled the man away.

Heart thudding painfully, Jessica sank back into the chair.

Cullen appeared and knelt beside her chair. "You've got to stop beating up on the members, sweetie. For a sub, you've got a real aggression problem." His smile disappeared, leaving his face hard as he scrutinized her. "Are you hurt at all?"

"No. I'm fine." Jessica ran her hands up and down her arms, feeling chilled. She saw the blonde doing the same thing. "Are you all right?"

Maxie nodded. "I can't believe you did that." Her eyes puddled up, and she sniffled. "You could have been hurt. Nathan can be really mean."

Jessica smiled. "Bruises heal. Watching someone get hurt when I could do something to stop it... That doesn't heal so fast." Like the guilt left from her sister. Her mouth tightened.

Cullen rose to his feet. "Maxie, why don't you come and sit at the bar for a while; let me keep an eye on you."

Maxie's mouth formed an O as her eyes went wide. Then she shook her head. "I can't, Master C. We're keeping Jessica company for Master Z."

Cullen's smile was back. "Dedication to duty is a good thing. Come on over when you're free." His eyes glinted with humor. "If you want."

Considering Maxie was almost drooling, Jessica figured the bartender knew quite well how much the blonde wanted. He strode back to his bar, his long legs a fine sight in tight brown leathers.

Maxie sighed.

Giving a cautious look around for any more overaggressive men, Jessica leaned back in her chair. Here was her chance at getting some information from the women's side of the fence. "I don't think Master Z would have been upset if you'd gone to sit with Cullen."

Maxie's eyes widened. "Defy Master Z? Are you insane? You don't talk back to him, do you?" She added hastily, "Don't *ever* talk back to him." The blonde seemed more scared than when Nathan grabbed her.

What made Maxie look like that? "But, Sir told me he never... He only s-spanked—" The word was difficult to even say. "He doesn't whip or anything."

"Oh, I'd almost rather be whipped than—" Maxie's eyes turned to Lenora. "You tell her."

Lenora sipped her drink then pointed with her chin to a tall, muscular redhead in a two-piece negligee who was sitting next to a thin male Dom. "Adrienne there was giving her Dom a bad time. She was basically topping from the bottom, not doing what he said, and creating a ruckus during their scene. Master Z went over. I don't know what was said, but I've heard she smarted off to him."

Lenora exchanged glances with Maxie, then continued. "His face... You know how he can look so deadly? Well, the Dom was pissed enough to tell Master Z to do whatever he wanted with her. Master Z picked Adrienne up like she was a doll, dumped her on her back on the end of the bar, and strapped her down with her legs V'ed up in the air. And he gagged her too, a good thing since she was swearing a blue streak."

Jessica tried to imagine being treated like that. On the bar? "How humiliating. I bet she never smarted off again."

Lenora shook her head. "Oh, it gets worse. He grabbed some vibrators and dildos, set them on the bar, and announced she was available to anyone wanting to practice getting a sub off. Anyone."

Jessica felt her own eyes going wide. "You mean...?"

Maxie nodded and almost whispered, "I think every Dom in the place took a turn. Adrienne came so many times that she could only moan for the last few."

Oh, God. Jessica wrapped her arms around herself. "He just left her there?" What kind of a monster was he?

"No, he wouldn't do that. Master Z's death on leaving a bound sub unattended." Lenora glanced at the bar. "He sat right there at the bar, sipping a drink and watching. He stopped a couple of the Doms when they got too rough. When he let her free, she couldn't even stand. But she sure apologized."

Maxie snorted. "She's been real polite ever since, you know?" Her grin faded. "But see, I don't want Master Z mad at me for anything. Uh-uh. I'm staying here like he asked."

Jessica couldn't keep her gaze from the bar. She noticed that the heavy wood ceiling rafters had chains dangling from them. God, she'd thought the medical room was bad.

"I think I'd die," she whispered with a shudder.

Lenora's gaze was on a group of three Doms sitting at a table, and it took a second before she responded. "Well, Adrienne likes the whip and cane. She was acting out partly to get herself whipped, and that was the problem. But Master Z found a punishment she'd do anything to avoid again. He's really scary that way."

"But he's sure something in bed." Maxie sighed, her eyes half-closing.

Jessica's head whipped around. He'd had sex with Maxie? A hard lump formed in her throat. "He's...uh, enjoyed a lot of the women here?" Her face heated when Lenora gave her a knowing look. She nodded.

"Oh, he's had a lot of us," Maxie said, then pouted. "But he never takes anyone for more than a night. Neither does Master D."

"And Master C doesn't go more than two nights, so don't get your heart set on him, dummy," Lenora said to Maxie in a dry voice.

"Oh, I won't," Maxie said and wiggled. "He's too intense for me long-term, but I'm wanting a little intensity tonight."

Trying to get the image of Sir and Maxie together out of her mind, Jessica looked toward the back of the room where someone was shouting. Two of the dungeon monitors were dragging a man toward the front. Face cold, Sir walked behind them.

Screaming curses, the guy kicked and struggled and suddenly broke free of the monitors. He charged at Sir.

Jessica gasped and jumped to her feet.

Sir knocked a punch to one side, and buried his fist in the guy's gut. The man folded like a jackknife, face purpling as he tried to get his breath. Shaking his head, Sir handed him back to the monitors, waved them off, and headed toward Jessica.

Considering the lethal expression on his face, she wasn't sure whether to run and hide or just whimper. She glanced at her cuffs. Running wasn't going to work. She tucked herself back into the big chair.

But as he approached, the deadly stillness disappeared. His eyes warmed when she tried smiling at him. He set a hip on the arm of her chair and pulled her close. And, oh God, that was just where she wanted to be.

"Lenora, Maxie, thank you for watching out for Jessica," he

said, his voice calm as if hadn't just punched a man. "I see you did a good job."

"Well, there was one little thing that happened," Maxie said, a quaver in her voice as she visibly steeled herself to tell Sir everything. Oh, hell. What if he decided Jessica had been out of line? Or decided to go after Nathan and beat the hell out of him?

Jessica shook her head frantically at Maxie then realized Sir's gaze was on her, and his gray eyes had chilled to silver. She froze.

His hand curled around her nape, holding her firmly in place. And damned if the feel of his hand on her, even the look in his eye, sent such potent need through her that she shivered.

"Continue, please, Maxie." Sir's voice was softer and much scarier.

"It's just... Well, Nathan came over, and he didn't bother Jessica, Sir; he saw she was chained, but he wanted me to go with him." She gazed at Sir with trepidation and whispered, "I said no."

"You have the right to say no to anyone here, pet. You know that."

Maxie's sigh of relief was audible and Sir's lips quirked. "He grabbed me anyway and called me a name, but Jessica kicked him."

The hand on the back of her neck tightened painfully before he loosened his fingers. Ruthless eyes pinned her in place. "Did he hurt you, kitten?"

"No. Daniel—I mean, Master D—hauled him away, and Cullen made sure we were okay. We're fine; we're all fine. Really."

His lips definitely curved, although the chill in his gaze was slow to fade. He let go of her neck and stroked his knuckles over her cheek. "I think later we'll discuss your need to shelter other women, Jessica."

Oh, hell, that wasn't a subject she really wanted to talk about. She frowned at him. Damn psychologist mind reader.

He tilted her chin up. "Did you just frown at me?"

She could hear Maxie's gasp and Lenora's hiss of concern.

"No. I didn't." She tried to smooth her face and ended up frowning at him anyway. "Really."

He laughed, deep and full, and the two women simply sat there and stared.

"You know, I think it's your fault that tonight has been so unsettled. I fully intended to have you pinned and squirming underneath me again, long before this, but Murphy's Law shattered that plan quite well."

Her mind played his words back twice before she realized what he meant. She felt herself turn red. And hot. And aroused at the image he'd set into her head: his body on hers, holding her down and—

"Z! Could you check this over?" One of the dungeon monitors who had been escorting the wild man beckoned.

Sir sighed. "Excuse me, ladies." He headed for the group huddled around the bar, but had to stop when a woman knelt in his path. A gorgeous blonde with a golden tan, slender and toned, with a perfect figure that the skimpy blue nightie didn't conceal at all. Sir spoke to her, said something, and the woman raised her face, gazing at him with a mixture of lust and appeal. No man could turn that down.

Jessica felt her heart thud into the ground at her feet.

Sir touched the woman on her head, stepped around her, and joined the men. Well, at least he hadn't taken her up on her offer right there. At least, being a gentleman—bondage and paddles notwithstanding—he probably wouldn't abandon Jessica for the woman tonight. Not tonight.

Her chest hurt, and she rubbed her sternum. She shouldn't be surprised. And she'd undoubtedly enjoy the rest of the evening. Wishing for more than this night from Sir was stupid.

She glanced at the other two women and saw sympathy on their faces. Damn. She turned back to watch Sir, enjoying the way all the men listened when he spoke. Nobody interrupted Master Z, did they?

He turned to take a paper the monitor handed him, and Jessica gasped. His black shirt was torn across his shoulder, the skin underneath covered in blood. Below that the shirt sagged wetly, though the red didn't show. "He's hurt."

And nobody was doing anything about it. Jessica pushed to her feet, tugged at the chain. "He's bleeding. Let me free."

Lenora's brows drew together. "We can't do that, you know."

Jessica growled. "You let me loose right now!"

Maxie's eyes went wide.

"You're an idiot," Lenora muttered as she released the chain, and Maxie unbuckled the ring keeping the cuffs together. Freed, Jessica ran for the bar, shoved her way through to the front, and slapped her hand on the top to get Cullen's attention.

He turned, gave her an astonished stare.

"Sir's hurt," she snapped. "Do you have a first-aid kit?"

He glanced at the end of the bar where Sir stood, then pulled a box off a shelf. "Go for it, sweetie."

Jessica grabbed the box and turned to fight her way out, only the people had moved aside, leaving a path between her and Master Z.

Intent on reading the paper, he didn't even notice her until she seized his arm and tore the ripped shirt from the wound.

"Jessica, what—"

"Don't move," she ordered. A slash, deep and nasty. Her head spun for a second. Blood so wasn't her thing. Then she set the first-aid kit on the bar, and ripped open a gauze packet. "You're bleeding, dammit."

He glanced down at his shoulder, shook his head. "Drugs and whips don't mix well."

"He whipped you?" Shock brought her eyes up to his.

"He tried. Considering he's still heaving his dinner out in the parking lot, I don't feel too bad about it. Serves me right for not being more observant." He touched her cheek with gentle fingers. "You were worried about me."

She dropped her gaze. Putting gauze on the cut, she applied pressure. "This probably needs stitches, Master Z." She risked a look up at him, realizing it was the first time she'd actually called him *Master* out loud.

His dark eyes burned, pinned her in place. He knew. He ran a finger across the top of her breasts and smiled when her nipples peaked. "Cullen," he said, without looking away from her.

"Master Z."

"I'm going to let my little sub finish her bandaging job upstairs."

Jessica's heart gave a hard thud.

"Please take charge of the club," Master Z finished, glancing at the bartender.

"Yes, sir." Cullen's grin flashed at Jessica.

CHAPTER THIRTEEN

Zachary tried to put his arm around his sub, but she took his hand and set it against the gauze covering his wound and ordered, "Hold that there."

He shook his head. From a submissive to a spitfire in five easy minutes. The contrast was startling. Compelling. Her concern spilled through him like warmth from the sun.

Until now, he hadn't realized he'd been cold.

Stunned into silence, he unlocked the private door and took her up to the third floor. Flipping on the lights, he waved her in, and got his first-aid box from the closet.

In his kitchen of granite counters and stainless steel appliances, she was like a beam of light with her vivid eyes and pale golden hair. Taking the kit from him, she started rummaging through it.

Zachary poured them both drinks then sat at the round oak table.

She picked up her glass and drank it in one gulp.

He managed not to laugh. "Rough night, kitten?" He poured her another shot, although gulping was hardly the way to drink Glenlivet.

"Take your shirt off."

His eyebrows rose.

Flushing, she hastily added, "Please?"

With a smile, he pulled the shirt off and tossed it into the wastebasket. He glanced at his shoulder. Not bleeding much, not too deep.

Lips pressed together, Jessica washed the slice clean then pulled the edges together with thin adhesive strips. She finished by taping a gauze pad over the wound. "I think that will be all right," she said before dropping into a chair at the table and downing her second shot of scotch.

He checked her work. "Excellent job."

She was still pale, so he poured one final shot and put the bottle away. Any more and she'd be out like a light. "Let's go into the living room," he said, lacing his fingers with hers. She had a delicate hand with small fingers.

Taking a seat in his favorite leather chair, he pushed the oak coffee table farther away and pulled her down to sit on the floor between his legs, her back against the chair. Her pale skin was almost translucent against the dark red carpet.

She turned to him with an insulted expression. "Is this where a pet sits?"

"No...pet." He put a slight emphasis on the word just to see her face flush. "This is where someone sits when they need their shoulders rubbed." His hands closed on her shoulders where the muscles were so tight he had seen the knots from across the kitchen.

"Ohhhh."

The sigh reminded him of her sweet moan when his cock entered her softness. He hardened, considered taking her right there on the carpet. But that wasn't what she needed from him right now. He dug his thumbs into her muscles, felt the loosening.

"Sir?"

"Um-hmm." He moved his fingers to her slender neck, sliding the cool silky hair to one side.

"I'm sorry."

There was a slight quaver in her voice and worry, almost fear in her mind, and he frowned. Sorry for what? She *had* snapped at him, he remembered, or maybe for the way she'd ordered him around? Ah, probably that. She was new to all this.

"Jessica, with some Doms, the slightest misstep will bring wrath down on a sub's head. I don't operate that way. That you were willing to risk my anger to care for me... Kitten, I feel cherished, not angry."

And the feeling was still so unexpected that he was having trouble finding his balance.

"Oh." She took a sip of her drink, wrinkling her nose slightly. Not her favorite drink. He'd have to stock his liquor cabinet with something besides scotch.

Under his fingers, her muscles tightened and he could feel a surge of worry—and outrage—from her. "I heard about the woman you...you put on the bar."

He bit back the laugh, kept his voice soothing. "No wonder you're feeling a little unsure."

"No kidding," she muttered, and he grinned since she couldn't see, and concentrated on working the new tenseness out of her muscles. She was just a bundle of nerves. And here he'd planned to have turned her into a little puddle of goo by now.

Instead he was giving bondage lessons.

Feisty, sensitive little sub. Then again, he'd never enjoyed teaching so much in his life. He wrapped his arms around her.

"Kitten, her punishment was for more than one misstep; she spent the evening deliberately annoying her Dom. And he knew that she'd find a whipping to be a reward."

"But why did she do that?"

"A sub who goes out of her way to be rude is an unhappy sub. She was daring him, practically begging him to take control away from her. If she had confined her actions just to him, I would have simply given him some suggestions. But she took that choice away from me."

His hands returned to her shoulders, easing the last of the tightness, even as his words eased the worry inside of her. She nodded. "Thank you for explaining. It suddenly felt like I didn't really know you at all, you know? Of course, I don't, not really, but —" She grabbed her glass and finished it.

"Mmmmph, there's quite a bit I don't know about you, either." Like why his little sub kept attacking Doms. He pulled her back so he could massage the muscles in front of her shoulders.

"Like what?" she murmured. With her worry abated, her emotions had turned to a warm hum, almost like a purr.

"You've been in the club two nights and attacked a Dom each night to defend someone. Instead of finding a dungeon monitor, you jump right in."

Jessica felt her mind go blank and she tried to sit up. "I... Anyone would do the same, keep someone from being hurt."

"Of course. What makes it so personal for *you*, Jessica?" His hands pinned her against the chair.

"That's—" She huffed out a breath. "Do I get to keep anything private?"

"Well...no." He kissed the top of her head, but his hands, flattened against her chest, didn't move. "Tell me what happened. Who was hurt by a man?"

Pinpoint accuracy. He must be a hell of a psychologist. And she shouldn't have had that last drink; her thoughts were scattered to hell and gone. "My sister. Her husband hit her, beat her up regularly."

"Did you know?" His hands were moving again, soft round strokes, soothing.

"I should have," she said bitterly. "I thought she was a normal newlywed, wanting to be alone with her husband. I believed her when she said she'd tripped on something or had a car accident. I should have known."

"Oh, kitten," he sighed. "Abused women will lie like troopers; they're ashamed, sure they did something to deserve the pain, or they feel that only losers get hurt, or they're terrified of their abuser. Don't blame yourself for not being able to tell. Did your sister get away?"

"Yeah. Once we knew what was going on, we got her out. He's serving time."

"And your sister has scars, doesn't she?" he said softly. "Inside and out and you feel bad every time you see one."

Her throat closed up at the sympathy in his voice. At the understanding. She swallowed, blinked hard. A minute later, she managed to say, "Damn, you're good; are you a psychologist or something?"

He laughed. "At least now when I find a Dom laid out on the floor, I'll know why." He gave her a little shake. "But, little spitfire, if I'm around, let me do it. That's my job."

Somehow he'd drained some of the guilt and warmed her more than the alcohol had. He kissed her cheek, leaned back, and took a sip of his drink. He was still on his first drink, and she was more than a little fuzzy.

Then, his hands returned to the front of her shoulders...and moved under her halter top to stroke over her breasts.

"I-I don't think there are any muscles there," she said, somewhat breathlessly as her body woke up and started clamoring for sex.

"Well, I need to be sure, don't I?" His fingers massaged her breasts lightly. He kissed her shoulder, his day-old beard scratchy, the roughness sending shivers through her. Her nipples tightened, and he noticed, capturing each one between his fingers.

Her body dampened, and she tried to turn, to touch him, but his hands kept her in place, and he nipped her shoulder. "Did I say you could move?" he asked, giving each nipple a pinch, sending shock waves coursing through her.

When he pinned her back against the chair again, heat washed through her. He controlled her so easily. He nibbled under her ear and sucked on her earlobe, and her insides turned molten.

"Then again, I could show you the rest of my home," he murmured, and pulled her to her feet. "I do have a bedroom." He led her toward the back of the house, past the kitchen, and a sound made him stop.

Jessica blinked as a ginger-colored cat stalked through the kitchen.

"Ah, about time. I was wondering if you were going to make an appearance," Sir said to the cat, kneeling to pet it. He looked up. "May I introduce Galahad?"

"Galahad?" she said in disbelief. That had to be the biggest and ugliest cat she'd ever seen, and she'd seen some monsters at the shelter.

"He's a very chivalrous fellow."

Jessica knelt on the floor and held out a finger to be delicately sniffed. In approval, the cat nudged her hand, curveted closer to be petted. "You must be quite a fighter." She frowned at the chewed-on ears and scarred nose.

"He's been with me about five years, ever since I found him raiding the garbage cans. He was big then, has grown even more since."

She would never have picked him as a person who would adopt a stray cat. She didn't know him at all, did she?

"Ben said you were divorced?" she blurted out, then flushed. Yeah, man-woman social skills were definitely not her strength.

"About ten years ago," he said as if her question wasn't unusual. "We married young, when I was in the service. Since I spent most of those six years out of the country, we muddled along well enough until I was discharged. After that, we both tried, but when I entered grad school, she called it quits." He quirked his eyebrows. "Among other differences, she preferred vanilla sex."

He gave the cat a final pat before rising, holding his hand out for Jessica. She let him pull her to her feet.

"And have you been married?" he asked.

"No. Nothing got quite that far," she confessed. "I never—" She stopped; she was not going to tell him that sex had been boring.

His eyes glinted like he'd picked that thought out of the air. Jerk. But he simply ruffled her hair before showing her the rest of his home. An office held a bulletin board covered with photos and letters from his pint-size clients. Framed crayon drawings decorated the walls. "That's quite a collection," she said, touching one photo of a gap-toothed pixie grinning at the camera.

He moved his shoulders. "I've been at it awhile."

And the children meant enough to him that he'd decorate his office with their artwork, she thought, recalling her colleague's offices, filled with business awards, pictures of famous clients, golf trophies.

"Two guest rooms there," he said as they walked down the hall. "And this is my favorite room," he said, showing her a room filled with older furniture, comfortably overstuffed couch and chairs, a giant TV on one wall, a piano in the corner, and a wall of books. She walked over to examine them: Sir Arthur Conan Doyle, Agatha Christie, Dashiell Hammett, Ross Macdonald. Her eyebrows rose; she had many of the same books. Her imagination presented an image of sitting on his lap, both of them reading and arguing over murders and red herrings.

Finally, he pushed open the door to his master bedroom. Dark blue carpet, mahogany furniture. Tall arched windows open to the night air.

A king-size bed. Her breath caught. Her body roused as if it had been waiting just for this room.

"I think you'll like the furniture in this room." His voice was husky as his hands settled on her waist, warm and hard and—

A rusty meow came from the kitchen.

Sir paused, sighed. "I have to feed him, or he won't stop complaining." He kissed her neck then released her. "The bathroom is across the room if you have need."

When he left, she crossed the room. She definitely had need, now that he'd brought it to her attention. The bathroom was gold and marble with dark green towels. The tub would easily hold two, and the shower could accommodate a football team.

While washing her hands, she glanced in the mirror and gasped. Mascara and eyeliner streaked her cheeks; she looked like a rain-soaked prostitute. She scrubbed it all off, checked the mirror and winced. Even with makeup on, she was just barely pretty; without it...

Scowling at the bare face in the mirror, she snapped the light off and went back into the bedroom. She could hear Sir talking to the cat, his deep voice sparking off flutters in her stomach. He talked to her the same way, she realized. Was she just another pet to him?

Her gaze turned to the bed, and the ugly feeling in her chest grew. How many of those women downstairs had been in his bed? Ben's words ran through her mind: *Women fall all over him, and in his world, he's known as the best master around. And that's according to the subs, who would definitely know.* Lots of subs apparently.

Would that gorgeous blonde be up here tomorrow? Jessica's hands closed into fists, but who should she hit? The blonde? Or herself for being so stupid and letting herself get more involved than she should have? He'd never indicated that he wanted her for more than just sex, after all. And she'd enjoyed the sex, hadn't wanted anything else at first. But every time she learned something about him, she liked him more.

She wanted there to be a *them*, but he didn't feel the same way. There was no future with him. She walked to the wall of windows and gazed outside. Black clouds were moving in, shrouding the moon and stars in darkness. It would be pouring rain before morning.

She wrapped her arms around herself as unhappiness twisted her stomach. Really, she should leave now; she'd learned the folly of driving on country roads in a storm. And there was nothing for her here.

She glanced at the bed, and her throat tightened. She would hurt even worse if she went to bed with him now, let him make love... No, what they had wasn't *love*, and that was the problem, wasn't it?

"Jessica?" He stood in the doorway. She caught the puzzled look in his eyes, the frown, and then he leaned against the door frame, crossing his arms and waiting. Watching her with an intent gaze. Master Z.

She didn't even know his name, she realized, feeling as if the storm had already started. No, she needed to get out of here before she made a fool of herself.

"I think it's time for me to leave," she managed to say.

His head tilted. "I didn't design my bedroom to make a woman sad, kitten. Or to make her want to run."

"I'm sorry, Sir. It's just... It's been a long night." Her chest hurt so bad she wanted to press her hands to it. "I'm going home now."

"No. You're not."

She blinked. "You can't—"

His mouth curved in a faint smile. "No, I won't push you down on the bed and have my way with you, tempting as I find the thought."

The image sent heat pouring through her veins.

"But I also won't let you leave while you're still under the influence. I wouldn't have given you any alcohol at all if I hadn't thought you'd be spending the night."

"Oh." Well, she probably had drunk more than she should have. But damned if she'd stay here with him. "I'll drive slowly."

His eyes darkened, the muscles in his jaw tightening. "I'll chain you to a wall in the dungeon before I let you leave like this."

The image actually made her dampen, and she closed her eyes. She couldn't stay in his rooms. Or go back to the club and be in that sex-charged atmosphere. "Um. Maybe I'll just go for a nice walk."

He shook his head with a hint of exasperation, then held out his hand. "Come, pet, I have a better idea."

She hesitated.

"No sex involved."

Why did his easy compliance feel so disappointing? "Okay." His hand engulfed hers, warm and hard, and just touching him made her want him more. Oh, this had to stop.

He grabbed a bottled water from the refrigerator, then led her to the back door, and down the steps to the backyard.

She frowned. "This isn't the same area we were in before, is it?"

"That was the side yard; this is the back. This area is only for my use." He tilted her chin up, kissed her. "It's very private."

God, he could kiss. By the time he pulled back, her arms were wrapped around his neck, and she was pressed against him all over. She felt so good in his arms—warm, safe...*stupid*. She shoved him away and took a step back, trying to control her breathing. "No sex?"

He chuckled. "I don't consider kissing to be sex."

"Kissing is sex." She glared at him. If kissing wasn't sex, she wouldn't feel so turned on.

"Since you aren't interested in sex"—he gave her a bland look—"you might as well finish relaxing." He led her past flower beds illumined with solar lanterns to a bubbling Jacuzzi. Heat rose from the water. After setting the bottle down, he pulled her nightie over her head.

"Hey!"

Ignoring her, he unbuckled the leather cuffs that were still on her wrists, then gathered her hair and twisted it into a loose knot on top of her head. Hand on her bare butt, he nudged her toward the water. "Get in."

Options were limited. Fight with him over her clothing or get in where the bubbling water would hide her.

The heat engulfed her as she lowered herself to the seat. The water splashed gently around her shoulders. Her wrists felt light... bare...without the cuffs. She knew he'd removed them to keep them out of the water, but it still felt like he was removing her from his life. She bit her lip, forced a smile. "This feels really nice."

"Good." He studied her face, a frown back on his face, then opened the bottled water, and handed it to her. "Drink this. I don't want you getting dehydrated."

As she sipped the water, he stripped out of his slacks in his usual efficient fashion. Standing on the edge of the Jacuzzi, outlined by the glowing moon overhead, he looked like a god. Tall, shoulders so broad, muscles rimmed in shadow and moonglow.

He stepped into the water and settled himself beside her. After stroking a finger lightly down her cheek, he leaned back, one arm resting on the concrete edge behind her head. An owl hooted from the trees as leaves rustled in the light breeze. The muffled sound of a car door, then a car leaving, drifted back into the yard. As the Jacuzzi burbled softly, Jessica let her head settle back onto the muscled arm behind her. She'd just let her mind clear, show him she was sober, and be out of here within an hour.

CHAPTER FOURTEEN

Zachary watched his little sub slowly relax, and the night's stress and turmoil uncoil from her muscles. Quite an evening she'd had.

One that had almost ended abruptly a few minutes ago. What had been in her mind up there in the bedroom? He shook his head. The ability to read emotions didn't always help with understanding. She'd felt desire and then confusion and...resolution. Yes, that was it. And then grief.

Grief as she'd said she wanted to leave. No anger at him, no dislike. He was missing some vital step in her reasoning, dammit. But he had gotten one message loud and clear; if she'd left right then, he wouldn't have seen her again.

He picked up her hand, kissed the fingers, and she only sighed. Letting her make such a decision when intoxicated and emotionally frayed... He knew better than that. If she still felt the same way when she woke, he wouldn't stand in her way. Although he'd damned well get her to verbalize the problem.

He *was* a psychologist, after all.

Psychologist enough to know himself and that he didn't want her to go. The opposite, in fact. He'd already known he wanted to see her again, but his thoughts hadn't gone further than enjoying her in the club. But as the evening had progressed, his intentions had changed. And when she'd bandaged him, warming him with her concern, he'd known he was doomed. He wanted more from her than a few evenings in the club. She roused feelings in him that he hadn't felt in a long time.

With gentle fingers, he pushed a damp tendril of hair from her forehead. She'd washed the streaked makeup from her face in the bathroom. Did she know how those tear tracks, that evidence of vulnerability, could pull at a Dom? She probably didn't even realize how pretty she was now, her cheeks flushed with the heat, her lips soft and kissable.

After she was half-asleep in the water, he pulled her out, dried her off, and tucked her into his bed, enjoying the way she unconsciously curled into him, soft against his side.

He woke before dawn with the moonlight streaming through the window. She looked just right, he decided, her golden hair spread across the dark pillows, her rounded curves bringing his bed to life. He shook his head, bemused by her presence. The tiny room downstairs was where he took his women; they weren't invited up here to his home.

But unlike many, she hadn't angled for an invitation. He'd wanted her here. Hell, he probably would have tossed her over his shoulder and carried her up caveman-style if she hadn't agreed. She was such a fascinating concoction: the sheer intelligence, the logical mind and reserve that buried her passion underneath. The way her insecurities mingled with that affectionate nature was endearing. Her loyalty to her sister, her courage... She was something, wasn't she?

Even Galahad had given his approval.

He ran a hand down the satiny skin on her bare shoulder and felt himself harden completely. He'd had a half erection all night, ever since she'd screamed in pleasure in the medical room, but she'd needed time to recover, and then whatever had bothered her had come between them.

Now, however... He slid the covers down, baring her. Moonlight gleamed on her breasts, leaving tantalizing shadows beneath. Her waist curved in, then out into lush hips. The darkness between her thighs called to him. His hands traced down her body, touching lightly, his fingers lured into stroking the soft breasts. Her nipples pebbled into points. Her breath quickened. The scent of her arousal drifted to him even as her eyes fluttered open.

Her body felt hot and needy.

Where are my pajamas? she thought drowsily, then more urgently, *Where am I?*

Blinking, she frowned as she remembered the club. Sir. A Jacuzzi. She'd been so sleepy. Was she in his bed?

Her breasts were lifted into hard hands, and she moaned as intense sensations rippled through her.

"Sir?"

"We're not quite to the sex part," Master Z said. "You may tell me to stop if you want."

His face was above her, the moonlight shadowing its hard planes. He smiled just a little. She was leaving him, she remembered. Wasn't going to do this again. Her heart ached at the thought.

She could call this one last time a way of saying good-bye, right?

"Don't stop," she whispered.

He took a condom from the nightstand and covered himself. "Now, open your legs for me, kitten." His deep voice was rough.

Her legs parted.

"Good girl." His hand touched between her thighs. She was already wet, growing more so as his fingers spread the moisture. One finger stroked her clitoris, sending fiery shocks through her.

She tightened, the heat rising quickly as if he'd already stoked the fire. She lifted her hips into his hand without thinking. When he chuckled, she felt her cheeks heat.

How did he affect her this way? She had never been so uninhibited before.

"I like the way you react to my hands on you," he whispered, kissing her deeply, thoroughly, his tongue plunging into her even as he stroked her slit below. The twin assaults left her body shaking with need. He released her mouth only to shift to her breasts, sucking one nipple, then the other, into hard points, and the tugging of his mouth tightened her core.

His fingers continued their slow slide over her clitoris, around and over until each touch sent her closer, until her thigh muscles tightened and quivered.

And then he opened her, positioned himself, and thrust into her. Her swollen tissues flared with his entry. He pinched her clitoris at the same time, the one necessary touch she'd been waiting for, and she screamed, her hips jerking against his as waves of sensation exploded through her, as her womb spasmed around his thick, intruding shaft.

He hummed in enjoyment, moving his hand to her breasts as he slid in and out of her very, very slowly. His thick cock and his fingers on her nipples never let her excitement quite die.

"I didn't think you ever made love in the normal way," she whispered, her voice husky.

He nuzzled her neck. His teeth closed on her shoulder in a light bite. Then he gently tongued the sting. "You miss being tied up already?"

Involuntarily, her pussy tightened around him, giving him the answer she'd never have dared to speak.

"Ah." His teeth flashed white in the dark face, and he captured one wrist, placed it over her head, and then added the other. One big hand easily pinned her wrists to the mattress. "This should do it."

144

"No restraints?" she managed to ask, realizing she hadn't seen any.

"Don't have any. I don't bring subs up here."

But she was here, she managed to think, and then he increased the force and speed of his thrusts between her legs.

She felt invaded and helpless to do anything. With her arms restrained, her body wasn't hers to control; she had no decisions to make, nothing to do except feel. Each sensation seared through her, the slide of his shaft exquisitely opening her, his hard hand keeping her from movement, his other hand toying with her breasts, plucking and pinching the nipples to just the edge of pain. To just the point where each touch increased her now consuming need.

Then, abandoning her breasts, he set his hand under one of her knees, pushing her leg up, opening her further. He began to pound into her, and the throbbing between her legs became overwhelming. Her orgasm ripped through her, hard and fast, an incandescent flame shooting through her. She moaned as she spasmed around him, as her knee quivered in his hard grasp.

And then his grip tightened as he growled out his own release; the sensations of his cock jerking inside her made her gasp.

"Ah, little one," he murmured. After letting her wrists go, he wrapped his arms around her, pulling her tight against him, his weight full on her and ever so satisfying, his warm breath ruffling her hair. The scent of sex filled the room. She ran her fingers through his thick hair and pressed a kiss to his damp shoulder. *How could she give this up?*

When he started to withdraw, she grabbed his butt, curled her fingers into the hard curve of muscle, and kept his pelvis against her own. "Don't leave."

He kissed her, sweet and slow, before pulling away. "I'll be right back, pet."

A moment in the bathroom, and he rejoined her, pulling her on top of him. It was apparently one of his favorite positions. He played with her buttocks, fondling and squeezing, the movements causing her tender clit to rub against him until she wiggled in his grasp.

He chuckled. "You can go back to sleep now if you want," he whispered, tucking her head down against his shoulder. His musky scent enveloped her; his arm lay heavy across her back, and one hand still grasped her bottom. She yawned, sliding down into sleep and safety.

When she woke, lying on her back, he was on his side, propped on one elbow, watching her with those silvery eyes. Sprawled out with no covers, she was naked to his gaze. She made a futile grasp at the sheet, but his hand came down on hers.

"Let me look," he murmured, releasing her after kissing her fingers.

Heat washed from her chest to her face, and she knew she'd turned bright red from the way his eyes crinkled. She frowned at him. "You're bossy."

"Yes, I am," he agreed, amiably. "Isn't it a shame you happen to like that?"

Huh. Hard to answer that one.

After donning a condom, he rolled on top of her and slid into her with one hard thrust. She gasped as the shock of the sudden entry reverberated through her system.

"All right, pet." Resting on his forearms, he framed her face with his warm hands, forcing her to look at him. "Now that I have your attention, you may tell me what was going on earlier."

His gaze was stern, his hands unyielding. His heavy body pinned her to the mattress with his cock impaling her. There would be no evasion, either mentally or physically.

She swallowed hard. She could get him to release her, she knew, if she demanded to be let free. If she walked out. The thought of leaving brought back the ache in her chest. She didn't want to walk out.

"Jessica," he said softly, "haven't we shared enough for you to trust me with more than your body?" His thumbs stroked her cheeks. She could feel him, hard inside her, not moving, but joining them together in the most intimate of ways.

But she knew how this would end, had to end. He'd lived alone for years. He had eager subs available anytime he wanted. Why would he change for her?

His eyes narrowed. "All that thinking going on. Tell me, pet."

Pet. Anger flared through her, even knowing he'd said it deliberately. She wasn't a damned pet to be taken home and then dumped at the pound if too inconvenient. Fine then, he could hear some truths.

"That woman who knelt in front of you? I don't like knowing she'll be here with you tomorrow."

He looked confused, but she couldn't hold back the next part.

"I don't want you to have other subs. Or women." And then insecurity welled up in her like an ice bath. What was she doing? Like he cared what she wanted?

She tried to look away, but he wouldn't move his hands or his gaze. The only thing that moved was his cock inside her, just enough to remind her of their connection. "Don't stop, kitten. What else?"

He held her in place so easily, and her wakening arousal set off another spark of anger at her body's weakness and at him for exploiting it. She glared at him. "Just one thing. *Sir.*" She almost spat the word. "There's more between us than just sex, and you'd see it if you weren't totally blind, dammit."

He blinked at her outburst. Then his lips curved.

"Spitfire," he murmured, his tone pleased.

"I—" God, what had she done? She wet her lips.

His smile widened at her confusion, and he brushed her lips with a gentle kiss. "It so happens that I agree completely."

"You do?" she whispered. There was air in this room somewhere, but she couldn't seem to find it.

Moving a hand from her face, he touched her nipple with one

gentle finger, watched it bead into a point. "I do. And I think it's time you gave me your phone number."

Her heart tugged inside her with the rising hope. She shoved it back down, trying to consider his request. Well, not a request, actually.

His gaze rose from her breast to spear into her eyes. *A command.*

"What would you do with my number?"

The corner of his mouth rose as he touched her other nipple. "Call you and ask you out to dinner. Talk to you somewhere besides in bed, much as I enjoy having you here."

The air was definitely gone; she couldn't seem to breathe. He wanted more than just sex? Wanted to actually get to know her? Or was this more of the domination stuff, only elsewhere? She hesitated. "Do I call you Sir at a restaurant?"

"No, kitten." Now it was really a smile. "I'm Zachary until we reach the club...or the bedroom."

Her smile equaled his. "I can do that," she said softly as joy filled her.

"However, right now, we're in the bedroom," he murmured, moving hard inside her, "and I do believe you just swore at me." The stern line of his mouth promised retribution and ominous amusement filled his eyes. "Give me your wrists."

Her eyes widened in apprehension even as arousal blazed through her body. "Yes, *Sir.*"

ALSO BY CHERISE SINCLAIR

Edge of the Enforcer

Master of Freedom

Master of Solitude

I Will Not Beg

<u>The Wild Hunt Legacy</u>

Hour of the Lion

Winter of the Wolf

Eventide of the Bear

Leap of the Lion

Healing of the Wolf

Heart of the Wolf

<u>Sons of the Survivalist Series</u>

Not a Hero

Lethal Balance

What You See

Soar High

<u>Standalone Books</u>

The Dom's Dungeon

The Starlight Rite

ABOUT THE AUTHOR

Cherise Sinclair is a *New York Times* and *USA Today* bestselling author of emotional, suspenseful romance. She loves to match up devastatingly powerful males with heroines who can hold their own against the subtle—and not-so-subtle—alpha male pressure.

Fledglings having flown the nest, Cherise, her beloved husband, an eighty-pound lap-puppy, and one fussy feline live in the Pacific Northwest where nothing is cozier than a rainy day spent writing.

Made in the USA
Monee, IL
21 October 2024

68452103R00089